Storm Constantine's Wraeththu Mythos

I0678447

ECHOES OF LIGHT
AND STATIC

For Alex

Storm Constantine's Wraeththu Mythos

Echoes of Light and Static

And Static

Book Two of 'The Gold Country' Series

E. S. Wynn

IMMANION
PRESS
Stafford, England

Storm Constantine's Wraeththu Mythos:
Echoes of Light and Static (Book Two of The Gold
Country Series)
By E. S. Wynn
copyright © 2017 Storm Constantine, E S Wynn

Cover Art: Ruby
Wraeththu Mythos Logo: Ruby
Editor and Interior Layout: Storm Constantine

Set in Palatino Linotype

IP0129

ISBN 978-1-907737-78-7

An Immanion Press Edition
http://www.immanion-press.com
info@immanion-press.com

THE HISTORY OF WRAETHTHU
A NEWCOMER'S GUIDE

(Updated introduction from book one of
'The Gold Country Series')

Storm Constantine

The novels set within the Wraeththu Mythos are published with the intention that they be accessible to everyone, whether or not they have read all of the preceding books and stories. This introduction is provided to give readers new to the Mythos an overview of the Wraeththu world and how it's evolved, and I hope it will also be of interest to long-standing fans.

The Wraeththu Mythos stories first appeared in print in 1987, with the publication of *'The Enchantments of Flesh and Spirit'*, which was the initial volume in the trilogy *'The Wraeththu Chronicles'*, but I'd written stories about these beings since I was a teenager. The book – when published – was described as 'ground breaking' because of some of genre taboos it challenged. *'Enchantments'* was followed by the final two installments of the trilogy: *'The Bewitchments of Love and Hate'* (1988) and *'The Fulfilments of Fate and Desire'* (1989). The books were published by Macdonald in the UK and TOR Books in America.

From the very start, something within Wraeththu – perhaps my own love of that world and its inhabitants – captured the hearts of many fans, who remained loyal to it, even when for over fifteen years I didn't write any new

Wraeththu stories. Fans kept it alive through fan fiction – creating their own stories set within the Mythos.

I realized I'd entered new territory for genre fiction with Wraeththu – a race that sprang from the ruins of human civilization after humanity had all but destroyed their own environment. Were Wraeththu the world's revenge on its savage, selfish children, or were they perhaps the outcome of a scientific experiment, designed to save the human race, that went wrong? The aspect that most set the book apart from what it might sit beside on book store shelves was that Wraeththu are androgynous – having both male and female physical aspects. While androgynes, or hermaphrodites, had been seen in science fiction and – more rarely – fantasy before, they had never been explored in such a way as I sought to explore them. Hara – as Wraeththu are known – have a deep connection with what we term magic, and are more powerful in many respects than humans, whilst also being deceptively waiflike in some cases. Warriors and sorcerers, farmers and diplomats; familiar roles perhaps, but robed in very different forms. Wraeththu sexuality is a source of power, an ability to transcend mundane reality as well as being an extremely spiritual practice.

When the books first appeared, eyebrows were raised, along with criticisms among reviewers, some of whom weren't sure what to make of the explicit and uncompromising exploration of sex between Wraeththu – known as aruna within the books. In those days, sex, relationships and deep characterization were not often a feature of genre fiction. Also, the relationships in the Wraeththu world perhaps seemed even more intimate and unsettling because I chose to write the trilogy from a first-person viewpoint – albeit through the eyes and mouths of different characters for each book. This, I felt, brought more immediacy to the narrative, and also drew the reader in far closer, but again – from my own reading within the genres of science fiction and fantasy – it didn't appear to be a common viewpoint to use in genre fiction at the time. That said, writers who greatly inspired me – Tanith Lee and Jane Gaskell to name but two – *did* use this viewpoint wonderfully and that obviously encouraged me to experiment with it myself.

Another problem for some critics was my use of pronouns, which often gave rise to misconceptions about the work. I elected to use the pronoun 'he' to describe hara. At the time, when I faced this labeling quandary, the male pronoun seemed less gender specific than the female version. Using "it" was out of the question, and while I played with new pronouns such as "ey" and "eir", these felt clunky to me and interfered with the flow of the story. Also, because of how hara initially came into being, the use of the masculine pronoun was more appropriate. More of that in a moment.

Some readers simply could not get past the pronoun and predictable prejudices came into play, from both hard-line feminists and bigoted homophobes, who could only see hara as a form of gay man. Some feminist reviewers particularly objected to the fact that only human males could become hara (initially). The term inception describes the transfusion of blood between har and human, and the subsequent mutation. How could it be fair (or even, gods forbid, politically correct) for only men to survive? Again, critics missed the point: hara were initially men *stranded* in a world without women, in which they had to become half female themselves. In his Gold Country novels, E. S. Wynn delves deeper into this

7

horror story for men.

Another difficulty was that the word hermaphrodite had fallen into disfavor. It was regarded as disrespectful to people displaying characteristics of both genders, who should be described as being 'intersex'. Personally, I felt the word hermaphrodite should be reclaimed, as it is not in any way insulting in its original sense. It derives from Greek mythology, from the story of Hermaphroditus, who was the son of the god Hermes and the goddess Aphrodite. Hermaphroditus was a handsome youth, who rejected the amorous advances of the water nymph Salmacis. The nymph came across Hermaphroditus while he was bathing and threw herself onto him, begging the gods that they should never be parted. The gods, partial to taking all mortal entreaties literally, transformed the pair into a single androgynous being. In later times, this term was then used to describe any human born with ambiguous sexual characteristics, or who displayed aspects of both genders. But the word hermaphrodite had come to be regarded as politically incorrect, and the cold, scientific term intersex must be used instead. To me, Hermaphroditus, far from being the embodiment of a medical condition, pinned down beneath harsh clinical light, personifies instead magic and love, as well as the swiftness and beauty of nature, and its unpredictable and shifting faces. Humans and animals appear in myriad different forms and variances; who has the right to say what is 'normal'? I didn't in the 80s – and don't now – see hermaphrodite as a derogatory term, and feel that androgynes in our world should reclaim it, as pagans successfully reclaimed the word 'witch'.

Throughout the 90s and 2000s, Wraeththu's fandom

continued to grow and thrive. I returned to writing within the Mythos with the publication of *'The Wraiths of Will and Pleasure'* in 2003, the first of *'The Wraeththu Histories'*, (followed by *'The Shades of Time and Memory'* (2004) and *'The Ghosts of Blood and Innocence'* (2005)). I've since written three more Wraeththu novels – the Alba Sulh sequence, which includes *'The Hienama'*, (2005) *'Student of Kyme'* (2008) and *'The Moonshawl'* (2014), and a stand-alone triptych of novellas entitled *'Blood, the Phoenix and a Rose'* (2016).

I started up Immanion Press in 2003 to publish my back catalogue and – as it turned out – the new Wraeththu trilogy in the UK. TOR books took the series for publication in the States. At the same time, having been introduced to fan fiction and finding some of it well written, I wanted to give something back to the people who'd kept Wraeththu alive and well while I'd been away from their world. I offered to publish the best of the Wraeththu fan fiction writers, both through novels and short stories. Any submissions we received would be elevated above fan fiction to become 'shared world', which is seen as more 'respectable'.

The first Wraeththu shared world novel was *'Breeding Discontent'*, by Wendy Darling and Bridgette Parker (Immanion Press 2003). This was followed by *'Terzah's Sons'* by Victoria Copus (2005) and *'Song of the Sulh'* by Maria J Leel (2012), and *'Whispers of the World That Was'* by E. S. Wynn, as well as a series of short story anthologies edited by Wendy Darling and myself. All of these titles are available through Immanion Press as printed books and also in eBook format.

'Echoes of Light and Static' is the latest Wraeththu Mythos novel and continues E. S. Wynn's investigation of

the world of hara. Writers always work with 'what ifs?' In E. S. Wynn's case, this was: what if incepted hara could not accept their new state of being and tried to deny it? What if such hara existed within a landscape that had for some time been isolated and estranged from humanity even before humans lost their hold on the world? What if...?

Many of those questions were answered in *'Whispers of the World That Was'*, and now the author takes it further, revealing what happens when hara of the most advanced tribe, the Gelaming, come across the hara of the Gold Country, where something very strange indeed continues to haunt the landscape and the lives of the hara who live there. E. S. Wynn – whose work has already appeared in three of the Wraeththu Mythos anthologies – brings a fresh new voice to the world of hara. This is a voyage of discovery – for the characters and readers alike.

Chapter 1

In the fading light of a purple dusk, I set myself down and close my eyes. Focus comes, settles, and as I reach out, I feel him. My chesnari. He's reaching for me too.

"Tule Wolf, light of my heart," he whispers, and as I open my mind's eye, I see him sitting across from me, cross-legged and smiling. I see his eyes, wide and full of life, cornflower blue under red brown hair worn short and wavy. I see him so clearly, yet in reality, he is over a hundred miles away. We sit within different circles, and yet it is the same circle, a place between, overlaid with layers of his land and mine. The stars overhead are the same, even if the whispering leaves of oak and pine that sprawl around him are not the coastal manzanitas and redwoods where my circle of fist-sized stones sits.

"Foxlight, light of mine," I whisper back. He smiles, and suddenly nothing around us matters. Nothing but the moment, the connection, the bond we share. It helps knowing that this is the last night we will have to meet in visions and dreams. Tomorrow, my Foxlight will ride into camp on a *sedu*, a noble white stallion with ice in its mane and a map of the otherlanes in its heart. Tomorrow, my chesnari will be here in the flesh, and I will walk with him hand-in-hand along the old road, which leads to the cluster of tents at the beach. Tomorrow, I will take him into the soft warmth of my tent and share breath with him for the first time in too long, show him the colors within my soul which I show to nohar else. "I miss you," I add. "How is the Gold Country?"

"We saw one of them today," he says. I catch the

11

excitement in his tone, the spark flaring there, and it brings a grin to my lips. "A harling came into Cinder Hill. Five or six years old, blue jeans, a spear made from a weed-eater bar tied with wire to a grinder-sharpened license plate. He had keys on a leather strap around his neck, like talismans."

"Did he see you?" I can't help the worry that darkens my features. "Hara like that--" I pause. "He sounds feral, Fox."

"I don't think he saw us," Foxlight says. "We followed him a short way, found his camp further up the eastern road. There's a tribe there, Wolf. They don't look feral. They look peaceful."

I have my doubts, but I keep them to myself. I focus on the connection, the vision we share in the moment. I focus on the features of my chesnari, his thin, strong hands, the remembered sensation of his touch on my skin.

"We're going to make contact tomorrow," he adds. "I know it isn't standard to make initial contact without a team of specialists, but I've convinced our superiors that we can handle it, that this tribe is innocent and safe to meet. I want you to be there. I want you to see these hara." I look at him, see the seriousness in his eyes and my heart skips a beat. "I'm sending a *sedu* for you," he says. "It'll be there by the morning."

I laugh to cover my nervousness. "I have duties here, my love. We're in the middle of a census of the delta to the south. I'm needed."

"I've already cleared it with our superiors in Imbrilim." He smiles, and I swear that in that moment, I fall in love with my chesnari all over again. "There are more disconnected tribes in Western Megalithica than we originally thought, and there aren't enough specialists to make contact with them all. There aren't even enough low-level scouts and census workers like you and I to meet them all. There's been a call for more support from Immanion for Imbrilim and for points west. You and I – we don't have to be alone anymore. We can work together, be the first hara to bring the light of the Gelaming, the light of civilization and peace, to the hara of these hills."

I almost lose the vision in the moment. I don't know much about the Gold Country. What I do know paints it as a dusty frontier, hot even in the winter, with flaxen sticker-brush jutting like sharp stubble from every hill and plain. I drift back to the gentle coastal breezes gusting over sand, the endless sea beyond a shore so close that I could throw a stone and hit it. The deep and inky blue skies, the towering redwoods of Megalithica's coastal northwest, it's all come to feel like home to me. It's familiar. I don't want to leave this place. I want Foxlight to find his tribe, make contact and then rush back to me.

"I'm losing you, Wolf," he says. "You're distracted." He reaches for me, and his hand half settles within mine. "Tell me your thoughts."

I swallow. I love him, my Foxlight. I won't spoil his excitement. I force myself to smile, summon a curve of lips that is wide and gentle. Focus comes back, and I can almost feel his touch, the warmth of his skin.

"I'll miss these trees, this shore," I offer, still smiling, "but I miss you more already, my chesnari. Send the *sedu*. I'm looking forward to meeting your new tribe, seeing the Gold Country through your eyes."

"Dream of me tonight," he says. He lifts his hand, and I meet it in the circle, press mine into it, palm to palm.

"And you of me, my sweet." I will the sensation of

touch through the vision, know that he feels it. "We'll meet in the in-between and hold each other until morning, and talk of all that we'll do and share when we are alone tomorrow."

"One more night, and it feels like an eternity," he says, shaking his head. "I wish there was time or a *sedu* available for a midnight ride. I'd give anything to find myself in your arms right now."

"Soon," I say, smiling wide. "I need time to say goodbye to my coast, to these cold and beautiful skies and the trees. There is so much here that sings to my soul, Fox." His eyes drift a little and I add, "trust that I ache for you, my chesnari. Trust that I would be in your arms right now if it were possible, but know also that this place has become my home. Perhaps it is good that I have a few hours to say goodbye before joining you."

"Bring something of the coast there with you," he says, offering a soft smile. "Show me the beauty of that place when you come."

"I will, but it won't do it justice," I say. "There is so much I'm looking forward to showing you when we share breath."

"And there is so much I can't wait to show you, chesnari," he says.

"Then we should rest," I put in, making it playful.

He nods, looks at me with admiring eyes, eyes full of love. With the end of the vision coming, suddenly he is holding on. He misses me, just as I miss him, and even knowing that we will see each other in the morning, it is hard to let go.

"Goodnight, my precious Fox," I say. For a moment, there is an ache, dull and unquenchable. I wish I could reach out, touch his cheek. I wish I could be with him tonight, but under these stars, these coastal skies. I breathe a tired sigh, almost laugh at how silly I feel.

"Goodnight, my joy, my Wolf," Foxlight says. "Know that I am with you now and always."

"See you in the dreamtime," I say, and as I look away, the vision flickers, fades. In the sudden darkness, the sudden silence, I stand and turn toward the sea. My eyes wander over the tents on the nearby beach, so elegant in clean, white canvas with brightly-colored pennants flapping at their peaks. Three hara in simple leather plate edged with gold thread keep watch nearby, and the light of the rising moon catches the chrome hafts and glittering heads of ceremonial spears. I hear the gentle sounds of a couple taking aruna somewhere in the camp, and it brings the edge of a smile to my lips.

Soon, I tell myself. *One night of sleep and I'll be with him.*

But I don't want to sleep and lose this place in the morning. I hesitate at the edge of camp for just a moment, then turn and cross into the woods, follow a familiar path through the trees for one last walk in the groves of my home.

CHAPTER 2

Sometimes, I can remember what it was like to be human. Sometimes, when I find myself alone in the dark, when I lie awake at night, when the cold of the coming winter begins nipping at my cheeks, my shoulders, I remember. It's hazy, doesn't come keenly. Remembering what it was like to be human is like looking back on a life lived in two dimensions from the place of a life lived in ten. The shades and fragments that come are always so flat, skin-deep sensations of maleness and male thoughts. We've come so far. We're so much more, now. We've come so far, I sometimes wonder why I ever look back.

Yet the memories come, floating and faint. Everything from before I was incepted runs together in a pastiche of pastel memories. Sensations, sounds, ideas and feelings. A past life, it feels like. A life lived in a different time, a different body.

It may as well be. It is, in many ways.

I shift against the goose-down mattress, the heavy quilt and silken sheets. Everything Gelaming is comfortable, even luxuriant. Past nights have been easier, even without Foxlight to cuddle, but with the coming day on my mind, exciting and worrying me, sleep only plays and flirts with me. It comes to me when I least expect it, never stays as long as I wish it would. I try to turn my mind to happier thoughts, to thoughts of the future, but something, a feeling, a sensation – something pulls at the edges of my mind, insistent and ephemeral. *Something is going to go wrong*, it says, and it feels like the coming of a storm, the promise of cold and lashing rain. *Something dark, just at the horizon.*

My mind wanders in the waking moments between shallow naps. Dark thoughts yield to memories of shadowy times long past. My final days as a human, my first days as a har. When the Gelaming found me, I was starving, lost, crazed. Three weeks out of inception, with no care taken to shape or guide me.

I remember that I was twelve when I ceased to be human. There was a small, sprawling city not far from the place that is now called Imbrilim. I don't remember the name, only that Varrish hara were always sweeping through, stealing and slaughtering. They'd come like a wind in the night, descend on a cul-de-sac or a darkened street, and kill anyone they could not carry off and incept. When they came for my home, when I heard them slash apart my mother, tack my father to a wall with knives and duct-tape so they could *fuck* him to death – I ran. I knew it was coming. I knew it was just a matter of time, and I knew what they'd do to me if they caught me. They'd *infect* me. That was how I saw it. Like TV zombies, they'd snare me and share their disease with me, make me one of them, violent and ruthless.

I had a route all planned. I had a way out of the city. I didn't think any further ahead than that. I didn't *want* to think any further than that.

Reliving it, the plan comes back with some clarity. I remember how I drilled it into my own mind. *The bedroom window, the three boards by the mulberry tree, cross the alley to the blackberry bush, grab the bicycle.* The street beyond ran right into the center of town. God, how young I was then.

It was terrifying, running from them when they came, tearing the bike out of the brambles while Varrish voices shouted after me. I remember the way my legs burned, the way I shrieked as I peddled, terrified, feet slipping, hands sweaty and shaking. When I reached the city center, I found it gutted and blackened, every structure burnt and open to the sky. I don't remember much after that. I remember cursing my parents for keeping me so sheltered, for hiding everything from me. I suppose I understand now. They thought I was too young. They thought that by denying the apocalypse, it might simply go away.

I think I picked a road and peddled until I hit something that popped one of my bike's tires. At some point, I remember the sound of motorcycles. I remember being terrified again, trying to push and ride my bike on rusty, bent-up rims, but in the end, I couldn't escape them. I was too weak to fight, too hoarse to scream, too lost to do anything but try to do both at once.

The hara on the motorcycles – they weren't Varrs. I don't know what tribe they were, what they might have called themselves. There were seven of them in all, a gang of leather-clad bikers who'd banded together in their new lives as highway hara. They had names like Mel and Jack, and the leader wore a vest of black leather embroidered with massive blue and white wings. His motorcycle was an *Empress*, big and loud. *A hog with pipes,* he called it. It was at his order that I was incepted, staked down to a heavy oak table with greasy rags and climbing pitons driven home by the chrome head of a hand sledge cut with Nordic runes. In a way, he is like the sire of this life. It is his blood that runs through my veins, even now, and it was he who named me. *Tule Wolf,* he'd said, drawing images from a vision he'd had. *Like a ghost in the reeds, watching, seeing in the mists what others do not.* I've never forgotten those words. They come to me anew every time

I have a vision of my own.

I can't help but wish I'd known him better.

It wasn't long after my inception that the Varrs came. I think they were Varrs. I'd known my gang of highway hara for less than a week when I saw the har who had incepted me cut down by a crazed shadow that was all teeth and hunger and hate. There was the sound of guns, the bark of rifles, and then suddenly the guns would not fire. I did the one thing I knew I could do. I ran, and the one moment when I dared to look back, I saw a dozen bodies bleeding on the sand beside the highway. Above them stood a har dressed in sleek black boots, blue jeans and a fur-edged biker coat. His eyes boiled hate and hunger at me. Seeing it drove my legs with renewed strength, and then I heard him howl, howl at the sky with a voice that still makes me shiver, even in memory.

My heart is racing, remembering that moment, the chaos of those weeks. Sweating, I throw off the quilt, stare into the darkness beyond my bed. Burying my face in my hands, I rub at my eyes, my temples.

Everything that came after inception I remember in startling clarity. I remember the road, the scrub brush and the trees. I remember the way I was pursued into the wilderness, and I remember every burnt-out house I took shelter in at night. I remember every chalky berry I picked from patches of dried brush clumped along roadsides, and I remember every rat, every ground squirrel and sparrow I caught and ate raw in those days. I remember the sound of hooves at night in the distance. The lights searching sand, the screams of humans and hara caught on the road.

And I remember the Gelaming. I remember when they came, when I saw them clash head-on with a gang of hara who mistook them for easy prey.

When it happened, I was hiding in the rusty frame of a stripped-down car. I remember watching the Gelaming, recognizing immediately that they were different. When the gang of harish raiders rose like jackals from the wastes, I remember the leader of the Gelaming group only stopped and held up a hand in a gesture of peace. He tried to speak with them, even offered them food and shelter at his camp. He was kindly, calm, but they wanted more than he was willing to give. They wanted the fight, and when diplomacy failed, the Gelaming gave them more fight than they could handle.

One by one, I watched the Gelaming cut down and extinguish their attackers. It was graceful, clean. In the end, the leader dismounted from his stallion, his brilliantly white *sedu*, and turned to face me. "You can come out now," he said, gesturing. "We won't hurt you."

That was when I met Arahal. That was when I learned that there were forces in the world that were not dark or cruel, hara who lived by law and discipline instead of by strength and blades.

That was almost five years ago.

I like to think that I've changed a great deal in five years, that I'm a wholly different person. In some ways, that is the truth. I have changed. I've become Gelaming. I've learned of our history as a species, and I've learned how to open doors within myself, fostered abilities that would have seemed like magic to the twelve-year-old human I once was. I've been tutored in the ways of aruna, and I've fallen in love. I've taken a chesnari, been bonded and talked with my partner extensively about building a life together, a life with harlings, with a garden and a home we can call our own. I've grown up, become fully har, and at my core, I know that the heart of that scared little child of the highway still beats strong and frantic. The mattress, the silks, the words we've invented, the airs we put on, the allegiance to this tribe -- they're all trappings, wonderful trappings, but they could also be ripped away in an instant, shattered and burned, scattered to the winds of this new world as if they had never been.

A gust of wind buffets the wall of my tent, whistles through the guidepoles and out over the ocean. *One army,* the thought comes clear, borne on the wings of worry and terror. *One army is all it would take. Sixteen of us here, on the coast, and only four in the Gold Country.* Our ideals, our purpose– they give iron to our hearts, embolden us to spread our light into the chaos, the darkness of a shattered Megalithica, but in truth, we are all so young, all so fragile. Our world and our ways are new, barely tested, barely weighed.

One army, the thought comes again, and I pull the quilt close against the cold. *One army built of the disconnected tribes of the west, and everything we are might be ground into the dust.*

CHAPTER 3

At some point in the night, the worries soften, break on my mind like waves receding into a placid nothingness. In the truce-like peace of the deep night, I sleep, wake only when the snort of a horse outside my tent reaches me, draws me back to the light and the subtle sounds of a camp rising with the dawning sun.

Sedu. I recognize the sound, the silhouette of the otherlane stallion. *Thank you,* I push the thought toward the horse, and somehow, I think it understands. It snorts again, tosses its mane gently, then wanders a short way from the tent.

Excitement builds in me again. I'm still a little groggy, but the promise of seeing my chesnari motivates me to throw off the quilt and start digging through my clothes. From the little that I know of the Gold Country, the robes of blue and black silk that I usually wear will be less than fitting. Out there, the heat, the stickery grasses and overall mobility will all be considerations that must be taken into account. It's been a long time since I've worn jeans, heavy boots and a cotton, button-up shirt. It makes me smile, pulling them on, imagining my Fox slipping free all of the buttons my fingers are fastening.

Working quickly, I brush out my long, dark hair, braid it up into a bun secured with a pair of chopsticks I carry with me mostly for the color. A black-shocked and stormy lapis-blue. Like my eyes, or so Foxlight tells me.

A leather satchel I carry when traveling takes everything else I think I might need. I outline the edges of my eyes with kohl, check myself quickly with a hand mirror, then toss it into the satchel too. Ticking things off my mental list, I tap my teeth with a finger, grab the little gifts I've gathered for my chesnari, then stand suddenly and step outside the tent.

The first thing I notice is the sky. It's beautiful, cloudy-gray and heavy with the promise of rain that may come only with nightfall. Marine layer, nothing more, but the air coming in beneath it is cool and pleasantly wet. I take a deep breath, then turn, notice the *sedu* looking at me expectantly.

"I'm just going to get some coffee," I tell it, pointing toward the fire at the center of camp. "Five minutes?"

The *sedu* snorts and turns back to the grass. Grinning, I hurry toward the fire, find a few of the other Gelaming sitting there. Tozna already has a mug ready for me, black and steaming. I thank him quietly, meet his eyes only as long as I have to. I know he likes me, lusts after me even. He's made it plain enough, but he's also been respectful about how I feel. I'm bonded to Foxlight; a bond from which I have no interest in straying, and I've told him as much on several occasions.

"You're looking stunning today," he says. "Robes, jeans, you wear it all well."

"Thank you," I shoot back, briskly, turning my attention toward my direct superior, a har with black, bristle-short hair and golden eyes. "Kiensa, you know about my leaving, I trust?"

"The message came from Imbrilim in the afternoon, yesterday." He hides his smile with a sip from his own mug. "I was told to keep it quiet until Foxlight had a chance to tell you."

"Sly dog!" I grin. "Are you certain that you'll be able to operate here with one less har in the camp?"

"We have five more coming in from Immanion tomorrow before noon," he says. "Go, and stop worrying about us. Your chesnari is waiting. Be careful, and enjoy the Gold Country."

I'm still grinning when I finish my coffee, hand the empty mug back to Tozna. The feeling of worry, of something bad waiting just beyond the horizon still lingers, still pulls at me, but right now I'm so excited to see my Fox that it's easy to push those darker feelings aside.

Kiensa breaks off part of a wad of pemmican and hands it to me. The taste is sweet and peppery, goes down easy, but when he offers me another piece, I politely turn it down. "My stomach is all butterflies right now," I tell him, and that gets me a laugh from all the hara around the fire.

"You two were made for each other," Kiensa says, tosses the rest of the wad of pemmican to me. "Here, for Fox. God knows what he's been eating out there."

Grinning again, I stuff the wad into a piece of paper in my satchel. I thank Kiensa, wave goodbye to the rest, and then hurry back toward my tent and the waiting *sedu*. Somehow, the stallion knows I'm coming, stands ready, waiting, eyes focused directly on me.

I lay a gentle hand on the flank of the horse, caress its ivory coat, as I turn my eyes back to the sea and sky. "Goodbye," I whisper. I worry that this might be the last time I see this coastline, these woods, feel this cool, ocean breeze. The *sedu* turns, nudges my arm insistently.

"Yes." I come back, blink, meet the *sedu's* eyes evenly. "I'm sorry. I've had a bad feeling about this trip since last night." The *sedu* snorts, and I pat his long nose in response. "It's not you, I promise. It's something else.

It's..."

The *sedu* waits for me to finish, but I leave the sentence hanging, let words settle into silence. I wonder if the *sedu* understands. Surely, it must understand. These creatures, they're otherworldly, something more than horses. Something much more than simple, earthly animals.

"Ah." I shake my head, turn back to the *sedu*. "I'm sure it's nothing." I force a smile, hold it, even though the *sedu's* eyes tell me he sees right through the facade. "I've got a long day ahead of me. You probably do too." I pat him again. "Let's get this over with, shall we?"

Another snort from the *sedu*, and I take it as an agreement. I'm not an experienced rider, but I know my way around a horse and saddle well enough, so climbing aboard for the journey is no real struggle. It helps that the *sedim* are so observant, thoughtful and careful. Like the few others I've ridden, this one anticipates my movements and bends a little to make the mounting easier. It takes me a moment to situate myself, but the instant I so much as think *okay, I'm ready*, the *sedu* begins to move. I can feel the *sedu's* mind touching mine, and then we're suddenly somewhere between, galloping sideways through space and time, darting like fire into the swirling chill of the otherlanes.

CHAPTER 4

There's ice in my hair, and a chill in my sucking lungs, as we punch back through to the heat of the day and the open, blinding sky of the Gold Country. Cantering along as if the jaunt through the otherlanes was no real ordeal at all, the *sedu* cleaves through the golden stalks of burr-grass, then slows while I struggle to catch my breath. My aching hands shiver in the horse's frosted mane, and then I hear a voice, which calls me back to the world, back to myself and the moment.

"Wolf!"

Hazy eyes blink, pull in the shape of a shadow, a figure. *Fox.* I push myself fully upright, struggle and half fall to the grass, as the *sedu* dips to make the distance less. Watchful, conscientious of my shakiness, the *sedu* walks beside me, lets me lean with one hand flat against its side. The burr-grass is almost waist-deep on me, but I push on through it anyway, can't help the smile already pulling at my lips.

"Wolf." Foxlight reaches me, sweeps me up as the *sedu* peels away to the side, stops a short distance away to watch us. Still limp from traveling through the otherlanes, I lean into him, grasp him by the hips as he pulls me in for a kiss. The sharing of breath comes sudden, fills me with light and fire, with the gratefulness and excitement and need we both feel. My eyes snap open as life shoots into me, and then I'm kissing him back just as hard, pulling him close, pulling at his clothes, wanting to rip them off.

I hear the *sedu* snort, whinny quietly in the distance. Fox breaks the kiss, looks up, and I can almost hear his *thank you* sent by mind to the otherworldly horse. Settling my head against his chest, I send my own sensation of gratitude to the *sedu*, watch as it nods, tosses its mane, then turns away, breaks into a gallop. In another instant, it is gone, flashing into the sky, into the worlds between worlds, bound for another place, another rider, another reunion.

"I'm so glad you're here, my Wolf," Foxlight says, pulling me against his chest. We stand there like that for a moment, connected and quiet, soaking in the sensations, feeling each other's heat and energy, the rhythm of hearts synchronized to the beat of the same sacred song.

"You are my light," I tell him. "You give me such strength, such hope for the future, such joy even just knowing that you breathe, that you love me."

"I'm grateful that I can say the same." He turns me to face him, looks into my eyes. "You are so beautiful, my chesnari. What I wouldn't give to tear off your clothes and take aruna with you right here and now."

"There's nothing stopping you." I grin back, glance around. "There's nohar else here, and even if there were, well…" I let my words trail off.

"Tonight, I promise." He kisses me lightly on the nose, reaches up to caress my cheek. "They're waiting for us back at camp." He gestures to the gentle slope of a hill that rises to the east. "Come with me. There's so much I want to show you, and so much still to do today."

I'm tired and still shocked from the ride, but his excitement is infectious, grabs me somewhere within and sweeps me up in his wake. As he walks, I fall in beside him, follow his lead to a place where the grass breaks and a little gravel path meanders toward that shallow, eastern rise. The stones are loose and the footing is shaky, but I make an effort to steady myself, reach for his hand only when I'm about to slip and fall.

"I missed you in my dreams last night," Foxlight says, leaning close, catching my hand as I stumble, squeezing it lightly. "I saw you here and there, in flitting glances, but you never lingered long."

"I had trouble sleeping," I breathe. I try to clear my mind, focus on the path ahead.

"Like waiting for morning on Yule eve," he grins. "I was excited to see you too."

I nod. "That was part of it. I'm worried about this new tribe you've found." I look at him, see the way he looks back at me, partly curious, but with an iron tempering his gaze. He's certain about these hara of the Hollow Hills. He's certain they pose no threat to us, to the expedition, or the Gelaming as a whole. I look away, gesture as I talk through my worries, my frustrations. "I have a bad feeling, Fox. Something in my soul says that there's a storm on the horizon, a building darkness that we are spread too thin to face as we are."

"Spread too thin? You mean the Gelaming?" He touches my shoulder, just lightly, offering reassurance. "If anything happened out here, if we discovered a tribe that was genuinely dangerous, Imbrilim would recall all of our survey and census groups in the far west immediately. You know how low priority our work is. It's just data gathering. Besides, there's a mountain range, a desert and a horde of Varrs between us and Imbrilim. Anyone without a *sedu* would be stuck here–"

"We're not invincible, Fox." I cut him off, and I hate the way he looks at me when I do it. I refuse to meet his eyes, to see the disharmony there. "We're gaining support in the Midwest, but don't let that sway you into the false sense that every gang and tribe in Megalithica will see us as a light of salvation. There has been resistance. If there's enough resistance…" I let the words trail off.

"No great reward comes without risk, Wolf," he says. "Every time one of our hara reaches out to a new gang or tribe, we take a risk. So far, most of us have been lucky. This will be my first, but I trust Phelu's judgment and he's with me on this. I think we'll be lucky with this group too." He squeezes my hand again, places his other flat against his chest. "I feel it in here, chesnari. In my heart. These hara are good. Even if they will not become Gelaming, surely they will ally or trade with us."

I make to say something, to voice more doubts and worries, but as we reach the top of the rise, he gestures again, calls my attention to what waits below.

"Look, Wolf," he says. "Isn't it beautiful?"

I blink. The sun is high and oppressive, but beneath it, spread out before us, is a land of rolling hills that shines like a mat of mottled gold. Dry, dusky trees rise up in clumps here and there like solitary sentries waiting for rain. A short walk down and to the east sits a trio of tents, very Gelaming in design, with white canvas and shining guidepoles. The curling smoke of what must have been a very conservative fire snakes from a circle of rocks in the center of the tents, and beyond it all, I see the black line of a forgotten highway carving through the burr-grass to a point beyond the hills, a point east that memory tells me must be the ruins of the town in the center of all this.

Cinder Hill.

"We've found evidence of settlements all through these hills," Foxlight says, wrapping one arm around me, pulling me close. "Most of the human towns and developments that were in this and the surrounding counties were abandoned and looted, totally cleaned out, but there were places like Cinder Hill that persisted on even into our age."

"But something happened, didn't it?" I ask.

"We've found a lot of bodies," Foxlight admits. "Piles of corpses, most of them hara."

"What killed them?" I pull my arms close, shiver despite the autumn heat.

"Men, we think," he says. "Humans. Probably organized military. Most of the corpses– they look like they were killed by a single gunshot wound to the head."

"Anyone can use a gun," I manage. "What rules out hara?"

"Nothing, I guess." He shrugs. "I've just never seen shots so precise with kills made by bandits or feral hara."

I nod. "Which is why you think it was human military. How long ago?"

"About five years is Phelu's estimate," Foxlight says. "Look, this is a grisly subject. Whatever happened here happened years ago. I mean, you and I were barely highway orphans when these hara died. If there were evidence of a genuine threat still present in the area, our superiors back in Imbrilim would have brought in a team of specialist field agents, the best of the best, and left us doing census work somewhere safer. It's calm out here now. The best people to ask about the history of this place would be the tribe living east of here, once we make contact."

I fold my arms, let my eyes drift back to the ground. I want to argue with him, want to grab him by his hair and drag him out of this godforsaken place he seems to have fallen in love with. The last thing I want is to go deeper, to meet the hara who live here, but...

"Come," Foxlight says, gesturing again. "We've a long walk ahead of us if we're going to reach the settlement before nightfall. Phelu has coffee and eggs at the fire. We should eat."

"I'm not hungry," I lie. Foxlight looks at me, and for the second time since I've arrived, I can tell that I've made him uncomfortable, even if only slightly. "I – had breakfast before I left." I force myself to uncross my arms, to be more open with him. "I'm sorry."

He hesitates for a moment, then pulls me against his chest, holds me so close, so tight that I know I'm going to have to fix my bun afterward. I don't care, not really. I need this, this closeness, this tangible love. I breathe, then sink into him. In the moment, I close my eyes and let myself melt, collapse utterly into his strong arms.

"I love you, chesnari," he says.

"I love you too, Fox," I try.

"We'll be careful today, I promise," he assures me. "No unnecessary risks."

This whole thing is an unnecessary risk, I think, but I keep it to myself. Going back to making survey notes about the edible flora and the deer tracks near the coastal camp I've left behind sounds far, far safer than trekking into the hills to meet some new group no har else has ever heard of. "Thank you," I say instead. "I couldn't bear to lose you, my Fox."

"Nor I you, my Wolf." He strokes my hair in the pause. "Gods, it's been too long since I've been able to hold you like this. Too long."

"Don't change the subject." I laugh, and after a moment, he laughs with me. "It has been too long," I admit.

"We'll have tonight to catch up on a few things," he

says then. "I promise."

"And every night after, if I have my way." I grin, get another chuckle and a kiss on the forehead in agreement.

Chapter 5

The downward slope of the hill is steeper, but my chesnari teaches me how to walk it, step-by-step with feet turned sideways, flat against the hill. At the bottom, the other three hara of his expeditionary team wave as we approach, and I wave back. Every one of them is dressed in the same basic cotton button-up and jeans that I wear, but they all look a little rough around the edges. That's to be expected, I figure, with all of the time they've spent in the field.

Watching them pick over the last of their breakfast reminds me of how little I've eaten, brings a spark of hunger back to me. Phelu offers me a plate, two fresh fried eggs and a scoop of some kind of local fruit compote. He wipes his big, greasy hands on his pants, grins wide as I thank him. I don't wait, but dig in immediately, take a seat on a round of oak perched near the ashes of the fire.

"Foxlight has told us a lot about you," Phelu says around a mouthful of egg.

I nod, distracted by the flavors in the compote. *Blackberry, cherry, peach–*

"Yeah, I don't think he ever *stops* talking about you," another har says, grinning as he hands a plate to Foxlight. I look at him, and he winks back. Out of all of us, he looks the most rugged, looks like the kind of har that would be happier sleeping in a ditch than a bed.

"That's Hursi." My chesnari gestures as he takes the plate. "He's our hunter. Good with a rifle and not much else," he teases the har. "Or so I'm told."

"I know a couple of *kanene* who could tell you different," Hursi laughs, then to me, he says, "he's just jealous because he can't hit a can at five hundred feet with a scope, even if his life depended on it."

"Yeah, yeah, brag and flex," the third har breaks in, shoulders his way between Foxlight and Hursi. Of the three, he's the only one whose jeans are stained with black grease. "So you're the one he's been waiting for." He looks me up and down, turns to my chesnari. "He's cute. You weren't lying."

"Twin Eagles," Foxlight gestures at the har, adds. "Phelu's partner. He's from the highways, like us."

"Yeah, but we're all Gelaming now, right?" He grins at my Fox, laughs. "Right? Eh?"

"And what do you do?" I ask him, meet his eyes evenly as he turns back to me.

"Electrics," he says. "Machines. While y'all are bringing the metaphorical light of civilization to the boonies, I'm wiring up the lights that make civilization possible after six PM."

That gets a laugh out of everyhar, even me. After introductions, Phelu wraps his arm around Twin Eagles and drags him off to the side for a kiss. Hursi raises his eyebrows, hooks a thumb at the display. Foxlight grins back, then wraps an arm around my shoulders. I'm too focused on the eggs and the compote to do more than raise an eyebrow, grin as my Fox leans in, plants a couple of tender kisses on the side of my neck.

"Alright, alright," Hursi says, shaking his head and smiling at Foxlight and I. "I know you haven't seen each other in a while, but we've got a long walk ahead of us, so save your energy for the road, yeah?" He turns, addresses Twin Eagles and Phelu, who are locked in a passionate kiss with hands that are starting to pull and rove. "You two have no excuse. I heard the aruna you shared last night and I was all the way down by the highway."

"But last night was *so* long ago." Twin Eagles laughs, raises his head to the sky as Phelu kisses him from his sternum to his chin.

"Yeah, yeah." Hursi breathes a mock sigh. "I swear, next *sedu* that comes out this way, I'm commandeering it and taking it straight to the nearest *musenda*."

"Hursi's right." My chesnari smiles, holding me close as he lets his eyes move from one har to another. "Phelu, Eagles. Let's pack up here and get moving. There'll be plenty of time for aruna games tonight."

"Unless this tribe turns out to be one of those prudish and puritanical ones." Eagles frowns, leans in to kiss Phelu's hair.

"Have you ever even heard of a tribe like that?" Hursi shoots back.

Eagles only shrugs.

"I'll start breaking down the tents." Phelu peels away from his partner, turns back to the camp.

Foxlight offers to take my plate and I hand it to him. Eagles sighs and fetches a jug, cracks the plastic lid off it and rations it out in bursts as he washes the skillet and dishes. Without a word, everyhar finds a job – even me. After Foxlight and I pack away his bedroll and tent, we help Hursi with his own packing, then hoof everything to a thicket of scrub brush just dense enough to hide it all. Phelu gets cunning with a trenching shovel, scatters the rocks from the fire and covers the ashes with dirt and flattened burr-grass. By the time we're done, there's no sign anyone hara or human was there. The area looks like animals weathered the night there, deer most likely, or free-roving horses, maybe cattle.

The supplies we take with us are simple. Venison jerky and more of that fruit compote. Phelu carries enough food for all five of us and some to trade in a canvas rucksack that hangs heavy from his shoulders. Twin Eagles carries a five-gallon carboy of distilled water on his shoulder, one weathered hand tight around the plastic neck.

I see Foxlight wave to Hursi as soon as everything is stowed and the tents are hidden. While the rest of us gather and check the straps of our packs, Hursi starts for the highway, a beat-up rifle wrapped with electrical tape in his hands.

"Where's he going?" I ask.

"Ahead," Foxlight says, almost absently. "He's our guardian angel. He keeps watch at a distance, checks the route for traps, ambushes, keeps us safe while we walk openly on the road."

"So you *are* expecting trouble." I look at him directly, study his reaction.

"Always," Phelu says, attracting my gaze. "It's wild out here, even with everything that's happened. Ever seen a cougar?"

"No." I shake my head, look across my chesnari at him.

"Think of a tiger, but in the pines. Sleek and deadly, same color as the burr grass. They keep to themselves most of the time, but they have been known to attack and carry off humans and hara."

"There are bears out here too," Twin Eagles says. "They're easier to avoid. They generally establish a visible territory. That's what Hursi's mostly keeping an eye out for. Bear scat and markings. Never can be too safe in these hills."

"I know this territory is new to you, and nothing like the northwest coast, but you'll be safe with us, I promise," Foxlight reassures me again. "There's nothing to worry about."

And yet I do worry. I worry, and no amount of comforting words from my chesnari will silence the fears that eat at me, trouble my mind.

"Come on," Twin Eagles says. "Let's go meet these hill hara."

CHAPTER 6

Once we hit the highway, we break into pairs, put about twenty feet between us. Foxlight and I talk while we walk, and in the breaks of our conversation, I can almost hear snatches of whatever Phelu and Twin Eagles are talking about. Words, or pieces of words. I don't know. I'm too focused on my chesnari.

"I brought you some gifts," I finally say, attracting his eyes to the satchel slung across my shoulder.

"Yeah?" He watches as I dig in my bag. The first thing my fingers find is a little scrap of fabric tied at the top to make a bundle. I pull it out, unknot the string, and he smiles as he pokes his finger at it. "What are those?"

"Blueberries." I offer the bundle to him, watch as he takes one of them between two fingers, studies it. It's nearing the end of their season in the northwest, so they look a little sad to me, but to somehar who has never seen them before–

"Blueberries?" he asks. "I haven't seen one of these things since I was a kid." I watch as he pops it into his mouth, crushes it between hesitant teeth. He takes a moment to swish it around, absorbing the texture, the flavor. "Wow." His eyebrows go up. "That's good. It's been so long I'd forgotten what they tasted like."

"I brought a bundle of salmonberries too," I add, handing him the blueberries and digging in my satchel again. "They're not as tasty, more tart, but I thought you might want to try them."

"Let's save some for later." Foxlight takes another blueberry, then ties the bundle shut. I slip it out of his fingers before he can shove it into a pocket and smash the berries. "We can share them with Phelu and Eagles over lunch."

I tuck the bundle back into my satchel, pull free the salmonberries and hand him one. Again, he's cautious, chewing and swishing, but this time he swallows almost immediately.

"Interesting, eh?" I smile, pop one of the salmonberries into my mouth. The taste is sour enough to make me shiver and I force it down just as quickly. "Gah," I swallow again, try to swish the tartness off my tongue. "I guess those are less ripe than I thought."

"I've got something for you too," my chesnari says. He reaches into a pocket and fishes out something wrapped in a shred of weather-beaten flannel plaid. Inside, I see a gooey-looking, coffee-colored wad. It's gelatinous and white-dusted, probably to keep it from sticking to the flannel. As I watch, Foxlight pinches a morsel between his fingers, pulls it free, wrapping up the thick trailing tendrils which hang from it in his hands before pushing it toward my lips. I take a lot of joy in sucking his fingers, cleaning the sweet and sticky morsel from his salty skin with strong, skillful movements of my tongue. He grins, watching me, enjoying it as much as I am.

When I finally pull free again, I push a ball of the stuff into my cheek, savor the richly sweet taste. It's the consistency of molasses, or even pine tar, and it sticks to my teeth, lingers on, tantalizing my tongue. "What is it?" I ask as Foxlight pushes a pinch of the stuff into his own mouth, holds it on his tongue, savoring the taste.

"Something Phelu made," he says, and we chuckle because it sounds like he has a mouthful of marbles. "It's like caramel. We found a couple of abandoned bee boxes that were packed with honey, so we uncapped and drained the frames. Only got stung a few times." He chuckles, pulling up the sleeve of his shirt, showing me a pair of bumps there, then pointing out another on his neck, at his hairline. "So Phelu mixed the honey with a syrup he made from boiling down the sugary sap of this local pine tree, then he spun it all in the pot with a fork until it was too thick to spin anymore. The result is this." He holds the bundle out to me. I'm tempted to take more, but the bit in my mouth is so dense I have a feeling I'll be working on it for a while. "He patted it down with some of the wheat flour he picked up in Imbrilim a while back so it wouldn't be as sticky, then tied it up in little bags like this."

"That's really amazing." I grin.

"I also made something for you," Foxlight says, smiling back. He hands the bag to me and I tie it closed, glance as he pulls something out of his back pocket. A piece of thick paper, folded to fist-sized. I slip the bag containing Phelu's invention into my satchel, unfold the paper. Foxlight grins over my shoulder as I open it. From the center of the paper, the carefully sketched face of a white wolf stares back at me, fierce but benevolent-looking, his eyes the same color of blue as mine.

"For my brave, yet tender Wolf," Foxlight reads the inscription he's penciled so elegantly into the margins of the page. "Thank you for helping me remember who I really am when I forget, and for relighting my soul with your love."

"Oh, Fox." I look at him, and in the moment I feel his love so keenly. I reach for him, and he scoops me up, pulls me so close that we stumble a little. Suddenly it doesn't matter how far ahead of us Phelu and Eagles are, how much further they get with each new step. All that matters is the now, is how long it has been since we've been close enough to touch, the connection when eyes meet eyes and the words *I love you* are said without sound, sent loud from mind to mind. Closing my eyes, I bury my face in his chest, hold him as he holds me.

"My light," he whispers to me. "My shine, my joy."

"I am yours, just as you have been mine," I whisper back. "My sweet, talented Fox."

"Hey!" I hear Phelu yell, and it makes me grin again. "Hey, you two! Keep up!"

"Thank you for the drawing," I say, pulling back a little. In the pause, I kiss him, try to keep it quick, but it lingers instead. Drifting, we lose ourselves in the connection, fall deeply into it. In the sharing of breath, I see thoughts that awaken the soume within me, images he's created of us and replayed endlessly in his mind in all the time we've been apart. The images are so intense, I'm struck by the urge to lay myself open before him right in that moment and reenact them. The thoughts, the ideas, the hopes – they hammer me like waves, powerful and full of need. I feel his desire, know it intimately.

And then he breaks the kiss, leaves me lost, floating for a moment at the edge of collapse. I feel his strong hands on me, holding me, but it takes me a moment to move again, to focus, to come back. When I look at him again, he is grinning, and so much wider this time. He knows what he has done, and he loves it.

"I swear to all that is holy that if you do that again, I really am going to rip *all* of your clothes off," I tell him. "I don't care where we are, who's around." I shake my head, let the sentence hang.

"Is that a promise?" he asks.

"It's a threat of the highest caliber." I lock eyes with him. "And I assure you that I am fully capable and well-enough equipped to carry it out, if need be."

"Feisty wolf," he growls at me playfully.

"Fox!" Phelu shouts again. "Wolf! Hey!"

"We're coming!" Foxlight shouts back, then to me, he whispers, "should I kiss you again?"

"Do you want to spend the rest of the day in a tangle of limbs here on the highway?" I ask him, my own grin wide, almost feral.

"It's tempting," he says, and I swear that in that moment, he leans in like he's going to kiss me. I almost lose it, and then he scoops me up suddenly and sets my feet flat on the weathered pavement. "Tonight." He takes my hand so gently, leads me toward the waiting shapes that I know are Phelu and Twin Eagles. "It's been so long since we've been together. I want to do it right. I want it to be truly amazing, with no distractions."

"Me too." I smile, lean into him. "Me too, my love."

CHAPTER 7

The highway that weaves into Cinder Hill is wide but rural. It's a curving, weather-beaten county road that expanded along with the cities it cuts through. Two lanes to a side in most places, but here and there it narrows to one. Not like the huge interstates and super-highways that rise under the sparkling waves in the Rift of the Damned or that carve through isolated stretches of the disputed territories. Not like the turnpikes that still stand here and there in the far east. There are trees here, tall firs and pines, evergreen oaks, buckbrush and the twisting, blood-red branches of foothill manzanita. With nohar to trim them, they crowd in against the roadway, push over the sagging power poles and spread their leaves as if trying to hide what humans left behind. It's enchanting, the way nature reclaims what was taken from it, but I also feel vulnerable. I think of all the threats that could be hiding in those trees, those thickets of scrub, berry vines and burr-grass.

When we break for lunch, it's on the highest point of a bypass that arcs over the eastern side of Cinder Hill. Foxlight points toward the crumbling buildings to the west and tells me of a day they spent exploring there, of all the old corpses they found, and the horde of strange, metal-armored manikins that seemed to clog every street, rusting to bronze on the pitted asphalt. I listen intently, chewing venison jerky and savoring another wad of that congealed syrup-honey confection while he tells me about the gutted buildings, how every strip of wire, every bolt and nail seemed to have been removed for some purpose none of them can divine. "So strange," he says, musing. "I have a lot of questions for the locals, when we make contact with them."

"How much further?" I ask, looking towards the east, following the curve of the road deeper into the hills.

Fox squints at the sun high overhead, then back west. "A few more hours," he says. "We're making decent time. We'll reach the settlement before nightfall."

"You think the manikins are ritual objects?" I pick at the chunks of confection sticking to my teeth.

"Maybe." His eyes stray toward the center of Cinder Hill. "I don't know. They had articulated joints, hydraulics. They were simplistic in design, like they were mass produced, but the level of detail–" He shakes his head. "They aren't stone heads or voodoo dolls, Wolf. They're machines, like robots, or something out of science fiction, but I've never heard of anyone ever coming in contact with anything like them."

"Maybe everyhar who did is dead." I follow his eyes to the western horizon.

"So who killed the machines, then?" He asks, looking at me. "I mean, that's assuming they were ever active. They're so rusted that I doubt they'll ever move again, if they ever moved before. Really, the only ominous thing about them is how many there are. There are hundreds in the streets down there. *Hundreds.* What was their purpose? They couldn't have been military, could they?"

"Those would be good questions to ask the hara we're walking all this way to meet." I glance at him. "Maybe it was an isolated test, a last gasp from the human military before everything fell apart. Maybe that's why we haven't heard anything about these machines."

"Yeah," Foxlight says, folding up his hands and knees

under his chin. After a moment, he looks at me again, watches me. "You getting that bad feeling again, Wolf?"

"It never left," I respond, and my tone is more sober, more firm than I mean for it to be. "It just gets stronger, the deeper into the hills we go."

Fox looks away again. I let him lose himself in thought while I pick idly at the last of the blueberries I've brought with me. After sharing some of them with Phelu and Twin Eagles, there are only a dozen or so left, and I fight the vague feeling of sadness that thought leaves me with. The Gold Country stretches all around me like a bright tapestry that is both gaudy and rough at the same time, and once again I find myself missing the forests of the northwest coast with a keenness that is impossible to deny. I don't want to be here, on the road, in this hot, hairy, bristly country. I want to be where the breezes are wet and cool, where the sky is always some shade of purple or gray. I want the *sedu* to come back for us now and carry us all back to the shore I'm familiar with.

"We should get moving." The words come suddenly, startle me out of my thoughts. Above me stands Twin Eagles, one rough hand brushing through his short, chestnut-brown hair. Foxlight turns, and they meet eyes in the silence for a moment. "You ready?"

"Yeah," my Fox says, blinks. There's a pause before he unfolds, rises, glances at me. "Yeah. We're ready."

"I'll tell Hursi." Twin Eagles turns, his eyes searching the trees. After a moment, he smiles, laughs quietly.

"Hursi?" Foxlight asks.

"Yeah," Twin Eagles turns back to us, "Every time I touch his mind with a thought to let him know we're moving again, he shoots back a joke. I swear he's flirting with me."

"He better not be," Phelu says, half smiling, hauling his rucksack back to his shoulders. "You're my mate. He can find his own."

"Maybe he'll find somehar intriguing at the settlement tonight," Foxlight puts in. Phelu raises his eyebrows, turns and starts walking. When Foxlight looks at me, he adds, "Maybe he'll fall in love."

"I doubt Hursi will ever settle down." Twin Eagles falls in beside us as we turn to follow his partner. "Hara like him – I don't think they're wired that way."

"Plenty of free spirits in the world," I say, and Twin Eagles smiles in return.

"That there are." He shakes his head. "That there are."

CHAPTER 8

The highway rises and rolls out of Cinder Hill, then flattens and cuts vaguely straight and steady toward the mountains. There's a subtle rise in elevation as we walk, but the incline breaks here and there when the road dips into a gully or into a one lane bridge sagging over a creek. Empty buildings rise from the brush at intervals, and in places the gravel has given way to more burr-grass. Even the asphalt is starting to crack and open for the thin, sage-green stalks of star thistle.

I pick one of the thistles for Foxlight as we pass, break the long, cactus-needle thorns from around the fuzzy and brilliantly yellow flower, thread the now harmless stalk into the curly hairs over his ear. He smiles, kisses my hands, tells me about some of the plants we pass. I learn that star thistle was an accidental import from the far south, hundreds of years ago. Fox shows me how to spot walnut trees and wild-growing Persian silk trees in passing, just by looking at the leaves. He talks to me about the ideas he's been gathering in his head, the concepts he's playing with for what to paint the next time he gets his hands on some decent supplies. Even paper and some charcoal would be a start, he muses, and I make a mental note to see what I can find the next time we're in Imbrilim or Immanion.

The trees clump closer and closer together as the road rises to cut through crumbling hillsides of loose, red clay soil. The gnarled roots of manzanita trees fighting to survive the steady pull of erosion stick out of the dirt like crooked fingers, skeletal and accusing. The sun dips to the treeline behind us, and suddenly I'm nervous again. The feeling is stronger here, now, in the waning sunlight. The feeling that something isn't right, that something bad is coming, something we aren't prepared to deal with.

Contact comes sudden, fluidly. We're on the road, nice and visible, with a canopy of live oak branches soaring overhead. There's a whistle, and then Twin Eagles grabs Phelu by the arm and they stop. Eagles holds up a hand, snaps his fingers, and a new feeling hits me, sharp and insistent, alien. After a breath, I recognize it as a burst from Hursi. It's more than just a poke. It's a *warning*.

I feel Foxlight's hand tightening against my arm, and then suddenly there are three more hara on the road with us. Bare-chested, dressed only in worn-out jeans, they melt out of the trees and stop in the open ahead of us, watching us with eyes that are wary, but not worried or threatening. I notice the handguns holstered at their hips. Old style revolvers, clunky, heavy, sagging on worn leather belts.

There's a pause, a moment when each side sizes the other up, and then one of the newcomers breathes, breaks the silence.

"My name is Ven. I am of the Thuulhuum." His eyes rove, fix on each of us in turn. "I've never seen you before. Any of you. What brings you to these hills?"

"You," Foxlight says suddenly, stepping forward.

I'm terrified when he lets go of my hand, but I stuff the feeling down, force it away. I want to reach for him. I want to grab him and pull him close, but I force myself to let him go. Ven watches his approach just as closely as I do, stays taut and wary even as my chesnari extends a hand in a gesture of peace. He doesn't match Foxlight's gesture. His hand stays at his side instead, resting casually on the grip of his handgun. "My name is Foxlight. Tule Wolf, Phelu and Twin Eagles are my companions. We've been looking for your tribe for a long time."

"And why have you been looking for us?" Ven asks.

"Curiosity." Foxlight smiles. "We're hoping to establish a dialog, exchange ideas, offer services, trade food, tools, stories."

"Are you Varrs?" Ven asks.

"We are Gelaming," Phelu speaks up.

Ven doesn't even look at him. He keeps his eyes on my chesnari.

"Some of us were from different tribes initially, orphans and ferals, but we chose to throw in with the Gelaming because we believe in a future where all of our kind are united in peace and plenty."

"You sound like missionaries," Ven quips back. "I've never heard of your tribe, but it sounds like we have similar ideas. The Thuulhuum were once scattered and only came together as a single unit after a great catastrophe."

"What kind of catastrophe?" I ask, risking a step forward.

"You carry no weapons." Ven dismisses the question entirely, looks each of us up and down in turn. I swallow my words as he pulls in a deep breath. "Nothing visible at least."

"We have knives and tools, but little else," Phelu says, showing his palms. "We are a peaceful people. The Gelaming avoid conflict whenever possible."

"Would you be offended by a quick pat-down?" Ven asks.

"Not at all." Phelu shakes his head, looks at each of us

in turn.

Ven whistles, gestures forward the two hara who are with him, watches as they grope us one-by-one. It's uncomfortable, but I can understand why they're doing it. I look at Foxlight as hands open and paw through my pockets, my satchel. I meet his eyes, and he holds the stare until I'm deemed safe. When they pat him down, I hug my arms against myself, give him only glances. His eyes are closed the whole time, his body surrendered and peaceful.

Even when Ven is satisfied that we aren't hiding anything dangerous, I notice that his hand is never far from the grip of his pistol. In the pause, he seems to consider us for a moment as if studying us, and then he finally steps forward, reaches out and shakes each of our hands in turn. "We get visitors so rarely that I can count on one hand the number we've shared a meal with in the last five years." he says, offering a slight smile. "It will be nice to have something new to talk about besides the orchards and the weather. That is, if you'll join us."

"We would be honored." Foxlight nods, shakes the Thuulhuum's hand. "We've walked a long ways to meet you and I'd love to know more about you and your tribe."

"Good. It's agreed. Over dinner, then," Ven says, gesturing to the other two hara standing silent on either side of him. "Spalsir, Jethi. Run ahead and tell the others. We'll need plates for four more."

Five, I think, but as I look at my chesnari, I realize there must be a reason why he has said nothing about Hursi. *Insurance,* I figure. Must be. Our guardian angel. A contingency in case things go wrong.

"We're very grateful," Twin Eagles says.

Ven looks at him, nods slightly, and I swear I still see

some wariness there. Not enough to worry about, but I see it nonetheless.

"We've brought clean water, venison jerky and some luxuries from our tribe that we are happy to share."

"If clean water is a luxury where your tribe is from, then please feel free to bathe in our river for as long as you like, and drink your fill while you stay." Ven gestures toward the road ahead of us, and his voice takes on tones that are almost kindly. "Follow me. Our ranch is just a little further up the way."

CHAPTER 9

My mind conjures all kinds of bizarre images and fears as we follow Ven up an incline of asphalt that curves around into a dark tunnel of black oak leaves and limbs. The foliage is changing here, lightening from rich green to brown. I find myself checking the branches, checking around the trunks, lagging behind while I watch for signs of movement, for signs of ambush. Fear creeps into my spine, my hands – and then Foxlight is there, taking my hands in his, smiling softly, leading me forward.

It's almost enough to make me trust. It's almost enough to put me at ease, but still my mind suggests movement in the brush, suggests plans, plots, dredges up campfire stories I've heard of cannibalistic hillbillies and backwoods rape cabals. We're underequipped for a first contact with a new tribe, probably outnumbered, certainly lacking in hara who specialize in fighting and diplomacy. I'm nervous as hell, and no amount of reassurance or touch from Foxlight is going to iron it all out. I swallow, try to focus on the road, on my steps. Phelu is walking side-by-side with Ven now, talking, but their words come back to me blurred, half-heard.

"Wolf," Foxlight says, and it pulls me out of the haze for a moment. "Wolf, hey. It's okay."

"I..." I pause, struggle with words. The rest comes in a whisper. "I know. I know. I'm sorry."

Foxlight squeezes my hand gently, pulls my head to his chest and kisses my hair. "No apologies, my chesnari," he says. "I've learned to trust your intuition. We'll keep an eye on these hara together. We'll be safe. Remember," he smiles, "we've got a guardian angel watching over us."

I know he's right. I try to put my worries out of my mind, focus on the road. It's maybe a quarter of a mile to the ranch, and most of that comes as a series of lazy curves that snake into the woods. When the trees start to open again, the road ends at the high gate of an impressive palisade all power poles and railroad ties interspersed with thin punjees of pine and fir. Each piece is maybe eight feet in height, and ground or shaved to a wicked point at the tip. The palisade comes right up to the tunnel of trees, and as we approach, Ven gives another whistle and the two hara he sent ahead push open the gate from within.

A little of my fear melts the instant those walls part and I get a look inside. Harlings run and play on the rolling green of pasture grass grazed low by lambs – that's the first thing I see. A rusty truck with a dirt-crusted plow trailer hanging off the back end. A ramshackle barn and weather-beaten houses, hara in simple shifts, sarongs, or shirts and jeans stop to watch, linger only a moment before continuing on with their duties. In the distance, a dog barks, and as I stare, a knot of chickens rounds the corner of the barn, pecks here and there in the stubbled grass, quiet and content.

"Come inside," Ven gestures, smiling. "Welcome to Segerstrom Ranch."

I let my eyes roam a little, take in everything that I can as I pass through the gate. I notice that the asphalt ends abruptly at the palisade, that the Thuulhuum have ripped up the road where it used to bisect the farm. I notice also that most of the houses look like they were built from local wood, hand-milled and painted in the kind of bright colors that were often avoided in human suburbs. The ranch is a commune, a collective, hand-built on the land of what must once have been a large family farm in the foothills. From where I stand, I can see that it had a house, maybe two, before hara claimed it. There are other buildings that look old, decades old, sheds and the barn, a place that may have been a roadside store, another building that looks like it might once have been a church, but there are at least a dozen other haphazard shacks and lean-tos on the land, with the lanes in between blocked up by gnarled apple trees that hang heavy with ripening fruit.

"Segerstrom Ranch," Foxlight says, attracting Ven's gaze again. "Where does the name come from?"

"It's just what we've always called it. Most of the hara here are locals who knew the Segerstrom family when they owned this place." He pauses a moment, looks toward the horizon, then at Foxlight again. "The last of the Segerstrom boys died a few years back, but we keep the name partly to honor them, and partly just because it's familiar."

"You haven't been inclined to give it a new name?" Phelu asks. "Something that sounds more har than human?"

"No." Ven smiles softly. "Other names have been suggested, but whenever it comes to a vote, the majority are in favor of things staying pretty much as they are."

"Your community is unusual for that," Phelu follows. "The world over, most tribes and groups have taken to renaming their towns and cities, casting off the labels of the past and embracing the new world we live in, the world we are building, as hara."

Ven's response is simple, comes with a chuckle. "Good for them. The humans of the Gold Country were often seen as being more conservative folks. I suppose the same holds true for the hara here as well."

"I heard we had guests," another voice cuts in. I look at the newcomer as he approaches, his strong hands wrapped around the handles of a pair of plastic buckets worn with years of sun and use. He looks young, maybe just past feybraiha and, as he looks at me, I see the string of keys hanging at his throat like a necklace, wonder if he's the har my chesnari told me about. "They look skinny," the young har teases. "You sure they don't have parasites?"

Ven hisses, makes a sharp gesture, then turns back to us. "This is Cougar. He was the first harling born here." He squints at Cougar. "He's also the laziest."

"You want to carry these fish up to the kitchen?" Cougar asks, offering one of the buckets to Ven.

"You're the har I saw in Cinder Hill yesterday," Foxlight says suddenly, interrupting Ven's reply. Both of the Thuulhum look at him and he swallows, struggles for words. "I recognize your necklace. You were out near the city center."

"You told me that you were hunting out near the old reservation." Ven's tone picks up a sternness, an iron. "What were you doing so far west?"

"Nothing." Cougar scowls at Foxlight, and suddenly I feel very protective of my chesnari. I close the distance between us, stand strong beside him, but Cougar doesn't seem to notice. He looks at Ven again, makes a loose, dismissive gesture. "Dad wanted me to check something out. He had another vision but he didn't want anyone to worry about it. He told me not to tell anyone." Ven raises an eyebrow and Cougar nearly explodes at him. "You can ask him yourself, old man! Go on! I'm not lying!"

"Dad?" I mouth the strange word at Foxlight, but he dismisses it with a simple gesture. *Old man.* Old terms. Terms I haven't heard in a very long time. Twin Eagles speaks up then, draws my attention back to Cougar and Ven.

"You mentioned a vision," Twin Eagles asks.

Cougar looks at him, and his lips part as if he's about to respond, but then he huffs and stomps off with the buckets instead.

The rest of us turn to Ven, but the Thuulhuum only sighs, shakes his head. "We're grateful to his hostling, and Cougar is a hard worker, when he works, but sometimes..." He lets the sentence trail off. "I knew his hostling before we were har. He was your average Gold Country guy, interested in beer, fast bikes, girls and not much else. A lot happened that twisted him up inside in the years after he was incepted by highway hara. He had a partner, a har named Stoff, but Stoff passed away before Cougar was even born, and neither one of them has ever gotten over it, I think."

"Sometimes there can be value in visions," I say, and when Ven glances at me, he seems to be studying me. After a breath, he nods, and I add: "I hope this isn't too forward, but may I meet Cougar's hostling?"

"Certainly." Ven nods, gestures to the east, to a place where the land of the ranch dips out of sight toward distant trees. "You'll likely find him by the river, minding the salmon poles."

"Thank you," I say. I look at my chesnari and he nods at me. Together, we turn toward the river, while behind us, Phelu indicates that he and Twin Eagles are more interested in following Ven, picking his brain about the day-to-day material movements of the ranch, meeting their leader, or leaders, as it may be. I pull my Fox close, thread my fingers into his, and then suddenly Ven turns back, calls out to us.

"Tyse," he says as we turn. "Cougar's hostling. When you find him, his name is Tyse."

CHAPTER 10

A pair of hara side-eye us as we make our way to the river, watch us warily, even as we wave and smile back. "Not everyhar is as friendly as Ven, I guess," Foxlight jokes with me. I smile softly back at him, gesture as the river comes into view. A single har stands at the shore, his back to us, one hand on the taut curve of a fishing pole bolted to a solid, concrete block. He doesn't turn when we approach, just stands there, as if waiting.

"I watched a lot of movies as a kid," the har who must be Tyse says, his eyes searching the darkening horizon even as we stop just a few paces from him. "Mystic Hollywood crap. Swords and dragons, druids and oracles." He turns to look at us, gives Foxlight the barest glance, but something in my eyes makes his gaze linger. "I thought about saying something corny and cliché like *I saw your coming in a dream*, or *I had a vision that you would come and speak to me*." He rummages in his pockets, pulls out a bent, hand-rolled cigarette, sticks it between his teeth. "Thought it might be funny, or might make me sound like some kind of wizard." He cocks his shoulder in a half-shrug, raises a lighter and clicks it in the shelter of a cupped hand until it finally sparks. The instant he lights the cigarette, I realize that it isn't a cigarette at all. The smoke from his first draw is acrid and skanky. *Ditch weed*, I realize. I wave it away when he offers me a toke. "Yeah," he continues. "It's important to make a good first impression if you want people to take you seriously. At this point, I've probably blown it."

"We met your son, Cougar," I say.

Tyse nods, takes another drag, blows the smoke away from us. "I heard." He gestures back toward the gate. "Sound carries really well down here."

"We were curious about your visions," Foxlight puts in. "We come from a tribe known as the Gelaming. Many of our hara have certain *abilities* that they have discovered within themselves, abilities they are learning to develop through practice and experimentation."

"I didn't catch your names," Tyse says suddenly, gesturing at us quickly with his joint. "You're a cute couple, by the way," he adds. "You only give off a little of that *I'm in a cult* vibe."

Foxlight and I glance at each other. When I turn back to Tyse, I meet his eyes evenly. "I am called Tule Wolf. This is my chesnari, Foxlight."

"Those are highway names, gang names," he says, fidgets nervously. "Where did you say you were from again? Gelaming?"

"We were incepted by highway gangs before the Gelaming found us," Foxlight says. "We are from Imbrilim. It's a Gelaming city, far to the east of here."

"Never heard of it," Tyse says quickly. "I thought all that was east of here was Varr territory, but you don't look like Varrs." He stubs out the joint, pinches it until it stops smoking. "You don't act like Varrs either. Not like the Varrs I've met." He pauses, sniffs. "Not that I've met many."

"You don't have to be afraid to talk to us about what you've seen," I say, and when he looks at me, I catch it again, that something, something that makes his gaze linger, something he sees, something he catches on that's in my eyes, beneath them. For a moment, his lips part at the edge of words. He hesitates in the silence, looking only at me, and I swear in that moment I feel like he's about to impart some great secret, offer up the images of a vision which will put all of my worries to rest.

"Dinner will be ready soon," he says instead, looking away. The joint goes back in his pocket and he turns, rubs his hands together briskly. You like bread? There's not a lot out here to make flour out of, but one of the guys makes a killer Indian fry bread thing with acorn flour. Little butter on it and, *holy shit,* I think I need some right now." He grins big, then hurries past us. I glance at Foxlight again, then watch as Tyse jogs toward the center of the settlement, doesn't even look back.

"He doesn't trust us," Foxlight says.

"It's more than that," I reply. In the moment, I mull over Tyse's words and actions, consider the way he looked at me, the way he seemed to look *into* me. *There's more there,* I tell myself. *He sees something. He's seen something in his visions and he's seeing it in me, or seeing something that reminds him of it in me.*

"You're right about this place." Foxlight tucks his hands in his pockets. "Something is off here. I'm starting to get that same feeling that you were talking about, that something bad is going to happen."

"Yeah," I say, but the word comes absently. My mind is elsewhere still.

Because for the moment, and for first time since I arrived in the Gold Country, that vague and ever-present sense of worry that has plagued me has finally gone silent.

CHAPTER 11

We linger by the river until the sun touches the western edge of the palisade wall. Before us, the pale blue sky yields to clouds that take on shades of rich merlot reds and visceral purples. It's beautiful to watch, the change in colors with the coming of night, the clouds thickening, darkening at the horizon, already heavy with the promise of rain. I remark on it and Foxlight nods. "The first storm of fall," he says, then smiles at me. "If we're lucky, that is. The Gold Country certainly needs it. These hills haven't seen rain in months."

Months, I shake my head, turn back to the horizon. It makes me miss the northwest coast again, the gray skies and damp, breezy weather that are the norm out there. Foxlight rests a hand on my shoulder, pulls me in close, and we stand there like that until the trees swallow the sun, leave us cloaked in the deep purple of magic hour.

Eventually Phelu comes to fetch us, leads us back toward the center of the settlement. I look around as we walk, take in the movements of the hara who call Segerstrom Ranch home. Most of the activity of the day has died down, and the residents of the ranch are already lighting fires, gathering in knots with bottles of homebrew, their harlings dancing, playing around their legs. Phelu leads us to a cluster of picnic tables, offers us a seat beside him and Twin Eagles. Already, plates and bowls are being laid out upon the tables, late-season salad greens heavy with the last of the tomatoes. Pine nuts, sliced apples and walnuts round out the meal, but the scent of frying fats on the warm, subtle breezes that blow past the shacks promises more than just greens. I start to salivate at the thought of meat, of bread slathered with sizzling butter. I don't have to wait long. Fifteen minutes, maybe, and suddenly there are platters of fried fish and slow-roasted pork laid out before us. "They've really pulled out the stops," Foxlight remarks, and I nod in turn, amazed that such a little farm like Segerstrom Ranch could have so much to share.

"They haven't had any visitors in over a year," Phelu says, already pulling fish from the pile with a pair of bent forks. "I talked at length with Ven about their operation here. They've worked hard to build a solid, self-sustaining community, a communal democracy in miniature, with no real centralized leadership or hierarchy. It's really fascinating. I'm looking forward to learning more about how it all works tomorrow." He scoops loose a chunk of fish, holds it up. "Who knows, maybe we'll learn something that will be of use back in Imbrilim, or Immanion."

"Just be careful," Foxlight says, and I can hear the traces of iron in his tone. "Keep an eye out for anything off." He gestures to himself and me. "We'll do the same. Some of the hara here are acting strangely. It worries me."

"Strangely?" Phelu asks him.

"Just little things." Foxlight's eyes scan the Thuulhuum around us, flick back to meet Phelu's. "The way they talk, the way they look at us. They put forth this façade of friendliness, of hospitality, but underneath it all, there's something darker. Can't put my finger on it." He shakes his head. "Call it a gut feeling. Wolf's felt it even before we got here, and I'm starting to get it now too."

"You're being paranoid," Twin Eagles says, smiling around a mouthful of fish. "These hara are a little backward, stagnant and human, even, but they aren't dangerous."

"And they have a right to be a little wary," Phelu puts in. "They've only just met us. I'm grateful for their overtures of hospitality, but we can't expect them to relax and trust us until we've weathered at least a few nights with them."

"I hope you're right." Foxlight glances at me, hesitates when he sees me looking around, studying the crowd. When I become aware of his scrutiny, I turn back to him, smile, swallow the chunk of roast pork I'm chewing.

"Tyse?" He asks.

"Yeah," the word comes quiet, almost bashful. I cut free another piece of pork. "I don't see him. I wonder if he takes his meals elsewhere?"

"Cougar's over there." Foxlight gestures as covertly as he can. I follow his finger, track the line to a table maybe two dozen feet away. Tyse's son laughs at something we can't hear, then leans forward suddenly, swoops sideways to bury his face in the dirty blond hair of a har that looks older, more seasoned and trail-worn than him.

"Looks like he has a friend," Phelu murmurs, leaning towards us.

"Might be why Tyse isn't around," I offer, though I don't believe it, not really. I'm almost certain he's hiding from us, from me, from whatever he's seen in me.

"Wine?" Ven suddenly appears, sloshes a mug down between Foxlight and I, then hands another to Twin Eagles. "It's peach and blackberry. More like a melomel, a, uh, a fruity mead." He grins, and I can tell he's already sloshed. "Grapes are a pain in the ass to grow up here, so we use what we've got. This is from last summer. Try it!"

I hesitate for a breath, then reach for the mug only to

have it swept away by Foxlight. He looks me in the eye when he does it, then takes the barest sip, swishes it around in his mouth.

"I'm sure it's poisoned," I tease. Ven chuckles beside me, watches for Foxlight's reaction. After a moment, my chesnari takes another sip, bigger than the last, holds it.

"I think he likes it," Ven says, then looks past him to Twin Eagles and Phelu. "Does the trick, huh?"

"It's pretty smooth." Twin Eagles passes the mug to Phelu. "Got more?"

"We've got a couple of carboys sitting in the cellar of the kitchen house." Ven nods, crouching beside us. "I think we can break out one more without anyone complaining too much."

I smile at Foxlight, wait for him to take another sip, then reach for the mug. He teases me by giving me a look like he has no idea what I'm reaching for, then chuckles and hands it to me. In response, I look him right in the eyes while I take a deep swig of the fruit mead. When I swallow, I take too much, sputter a little at the burn.

"Hey now, it isn't that bad, is it?" Ven laughs, claps me on the back. I shake my head, take a smaller sip and then nod in approval.

"It's–" I clear my throat. "It's actually really good."

"I'll go get that other carboy, then." Ven stands, stumbles off, leaves us grinning.

"We have a lot to celebrate tonight," somehar else says, calling out over the noise around the tables. I follow Foxlight's gaze to the source, see a har standing on one of the tables with a ceramic mug raised high. I don't recognize him, so I lean in toward Eagles, gesture.

"Heggstadt," Eagles whispers back. All around us, the hara of Segerstrom Ranch are going quiet, ending conversations, turning their attention to the har we're talking about. "Phelu and I met him when we arrived. He's like a counselor, or a master of ceremonies. He handles disagreements and coordinates celebrations, that kind of thing. Can't really call him one of the ranch's leaders. Everyhar here is in charge of something."

"We have a lot to celebrate tonight," Heggstadt says again, addressing everyhar as the last voice falls silent. "It has been a dry year. It has been a hard year. We've lost livestock to the bears and mountain lions. Tildir and Honaan lost their son to a pack of wild dogs." He lets the words sink in as the silence deepens. "This summer, the river got so low that some worried it might thin to a trickle before the rains would come. The river is our lifeblood. Its water is the base upon which all that we have is built. It nourishes our crops, gives us fish to eat and grows the fodder that keeps our pigs and sheep fat."

Heggstadt pauses again, climbs down from the table to stand more evenly and equally with his tribe. "Tonight," he says, gesturing at the sky, at the ranch, "our fortunes change. Tonight, there will be rain, and snow in the mountains." A cheer starts, but he speaks louder, cuts it off before it can blossom into more than a rumble. "Tonight, the dry days of summer end, and the first rains of fall begin. Tonight, we celebrate not just the turning of the wheel to the autumn season, but also the promise of good fortune that I know you can all feel coming. We have guests for the first time since last Spring!" He gestures at our table, grins at us. "Guests who come from a prosperous tribe far from here that wishes to bring peace and trade to our people, and if that isn't a good omen, then I don't know what is!"

The applause is thunderous. Amidst the cheering,

hooting and clapping, Heggstadt thrusts his mug in the air again, announces, "To Segerstrom Ranch!"

"To Segerstrom Ranch!" Everyhar cheers. Even Foxlight and I are swept up into the pull of the moment, raising fists instead of mugs.

"To the rains!" Heggstadt calls for another cheer, and it's echoed as loudly as the last. "To the Gelaming! To the future!"

It's infectious, his drunken enthusiasm, his excitement. Foxlight and I watch in amazement as Twin Eagles clambers onto the table, holds his own mug high in the air.

"To the Thuulhuum!" He shotguns his wine as the cheer rises around him. I shake my head, laugh a little as the sweet melomel runs down the sides of his mouth, drips onto his shirt. Other hara start making their own cheers, their own toasts, and soon, the whole party turns into a chaos of laughter and shouting. In the midst of it all, somehar starts drumming, and then others join in. The night becomes a celebration cast in the orange flickers of bonfire light and wrapped in a soundtrack of drums, acoustic guitars and rattles that somehow seems to flow together, synchronize into an impressive rhythm as the night goes on.

Or maybe it only seems that way because of the wine. Ven, sweet fellow that he is, keeps our mugs full. When Foxlight finally takes my arm and leads me off to a little shack that Phelu and the hara of Segerstrom Ranch have arranged to be set aside for us to stay in, I stumble to keep up with him, grinning the whole way.

I think I'm the first one to get naked. I don't know. All I know is that I feel him, insistent and hungry against my skin, firmly ouana. Like water, I take him, pull him to the bed and flow around him, warm and welcoming. I draw him into an ocean of soume, let him rise within me and carry me, wild and strong. Above me, he is like a stallion of fire and need too long denied. My lips seek his and when they lock suddenly, we share breath in a chaotic flex of sound, sensations and images. It hits me with enough force to nearly knock me loose from the moorings of my material body, and in the sharing I see all that he has kept inside since I've last seen him. All the fantasies, all the hunger, all the doubts in their cages, now unlocked and set free. With arms and legs, I pull him closer, hold him as he bucks, shakes free all that he is and rises toward a quick, violent release. Taut as a wire, it moves like a current within him, as much electric as it is like a river. My hands seize his back, his hips, and then I catch him as he falls, fills me with it, sheds all that he is in an animal torrent that comes with a howl and the sudden surrender of seed.

And in the sweet thereafter, we float back to who we are on wings of sweat and broken breath. Notions of masculine and feminine fade and we become again two beings who simply *are*, two souls clad in flesh that is neither male nor female, yet both at the same time. My chesnari buries his face into the pillow beside me as I pull him close, shelter him with my body, my arms. Beyond the walls of our shack, I hear the sounds of the party as they crumble and fade beneath the quickening rain, until they are no more, until there is only the steady drum and thunder of the storm. In the quiet we share, insulated by the walls of the shack and the steady rhythm of the rain, I caress my chesnari's cheek until he falls asleep beside me, then tuck myself into his hair, breathe his welcome scent until I join him to play in dreams in the land beyond.

CHAPTER 12

When I wake, I wake with a start. It's dark, completely dark, and the night is dead silent. Even the sound of the rain has gone. I wait, lie there, just listening, parsing silence for even the sounds of crickets–

And then I hear it, a subtle crack and click at the door of the shack. Every hair stands up on end, and I search the bed for sign of my Foxlight, but there is nothing, *no har.* I tense in the silence, listen intently. The door opens, and there's a shape at the threshold. The scuff of a foot against the frame. "Fox?" I whisper, and the figure pauses, lets the silence hang for a moment.

"No." The voice is har, familiar, but unplaceable. My hands tighten in the sheets of the bed, and suddenly my mind kicks into overdrive, terrified and ready to fight. "It's me. It's Tyse."

Tyse? That doesn't make it better. I bare teeth at the darkness, but he doesn't come any closer.

"Where is my chesnari?" I growl, loud and fierce.

"In the kitchen-house," Tyse replies. "He got up to take a piss. I ran into him while he was walking the grounds. He said he couldn't sleep, so I showed him where the leftovers from dinner are."

I roll Tyse's words through my mind for a moment. It doesn't sound unlike Foxlight to wake with worries and try to walk them off in the night. I breathe a little easier, but my muscles are still tense.

And then there's a sound, a deep, distant call that chills my blood the instant I hear it. A sound like a shout mixed with a cough, deep and throaty. "What is that?" I whisper.

"Mountain lion," Tyse says. "She's calling to us." He pauses, then adds. "Put on your clothes. There's something I want to show you."

Tyse doesn't give me time for more. The door closes and leaves me in total darkness again. Absently, I reach up, pull free the one chopstick still tangled in my hair and do my best to brush the knots out with my fingers. Searching by feel, I manage to find pants, a shirt. I think they're mine. The shirt feels a little tight. Might be Foxlight's.

When I cross out into the night air, I spot Tyse immediately by the cherry of his joint. He's standing at the corner of another shack a few dozen feet away, and I can smell the stink of the ditch weed mingled with the sweet, cool air that follows the cleansing wash of a storm. In the dimness, I see a shift of movement, realize he's gesturing to me. In the time it takes me to cross over to him, he's stubbed out the joint again, expelled the last of the smoke.

"What did you want to show me?" I ask him. I can almost see his face in the scant light, and I think he raises his eyebrows. He's shivering, and when the mountain lion calls again, he points in the direction of the call.

"You wanted to know about my visions," he says. "She comes when there's a vision to share. She's calling to us. She's calling to both of us."

I look toward the palisade that surrounds Segerstrom Ranch and I stare into the towering trees and inky night. Part of me wants to call bullshit on the whole thing, but another part of me knows it isn't a lie. It would be ignorant, stupid even, to dismiss Tyse's visions as madness, or the call, the presence of a mountain lion as a guide as nothing more than simple delusion. *Everything happens for a reason,* I tell myself. Everything I've felt has led me to this moment, in this place, with this har who has something to teach me. I pull in a shaky breath, push my hands into my pockets and nod.

"Okay," I swallow. "I'm ready."

Tyse says nothing. He turns instead and walks toward the distant wall, toward the trees and the night. I stumble here and there, trying to keep up with him, but he knows the land better than I do. Like ghosts, we descend the incline which moves toward the river, walk along the shore on a trail edged with blackberry brambles, and then cut north-east through an orchard of towering, ancient-looking apple trees. The further out we go, the taller the burr-grass gets, and by the time we reach the far wall, the stalks are waist-high, swept downward like wet hair and sagging with so much rain that merely crossing through it soaks us to the skin. When we reach the palisade, Tyse shoves at one of the power pole supports, reveals a door on hidden hinges blocked by a substantial thicket of brambles and buckbrush on the other side. "Back door," he says as he holds it open for me. He clicks his lighter and uses the flame to show me a dip in the dirt that goes under the brambles, with just enough room for somehar to crawl through on hands and knees. The lighter goes out, and Tyse squeezes past me, wriggles over damp leaves and loamy earth, disappears into the darkness.

I do my best to keep up with him, eventually we tunnel out of the thorns and brush and emerge into the light again. Standing up, I hear him take in a deep breath, shift and go silent. The barest sound of crickets chirping in the night reaches us, and then I hear the mountain lion again, way in the distance.

Tyse doesn't wait. He's off like a shot, hurling himself

toward the call, toward the lioness. It takes everything I can do not to trip or run into trees that rise out of the darkness as I chase him. Branches whip past, lash and cut me, and through it all, somehow, I find his hand, and everything seems to jump to light speed in that moment. The woods whip past impossibly fast, trees and brush invisible until they're rushing by, gone again in an instant. To me, it seems like we clear miles in mere seconds, and I wonder if maybe we are, if Tyse might be skipping across the surface of the otherlanes like a rock across a pond.

Seconds, and it ends. I feel Tyse let go as we crash into a clearing, a meadow of soft grass and sodden soil crisscrossed by a web of clear-running creeks. He stumbles to a stop a handful of feet from me, yells loud and feral, and I see a shape move in response, turn and stare directly at us.

No, not at us, I realize. *At me.*

The clouds part and roll away with surreal swiftness, and in the light of the moon and stars I see her – the lioness, regal and dun-colored. Her golden eyes look into mine, and in the moment I can hear her, can hear the voices that she hears.

"Do you hear them?" Tyse shouts back at me, and I can only nod. My eyes never leave those of the mother cougar. Her words snare me, fill me, the words of a thousand voices all talking at once, shouting for my attention, weaving in and out of one another to build castles of color and memory in my mind. In the wash of words, I lose myself, feel myself swept up, and then Tyse is there, holding me, looking into my eyes, searching for answers.

As quickly as it came, the tide of voices recedes then, falls away until there is nothing but a mental echo and silence. I fight to catch my breath, and between gasps I hear the mountain lion call again, distant and lonely. The voices she's left in my mind stir only as whispers now, but as Tyse leans in, I know he has heard them too. The clouds above him have sealed over again, closed like a wound, as seamless as if they had never parted.

"You saw the dragon?" He asks suddenly.

I think back, think back to the voices, the images that rose out of them.

In the pause, he gets insistent. "The brass dragon?"

"I saw." I squint, raise one weak hand to rub at my forehead. "I don't know what I saw. It was blurry, strange, broken."

Tyse swoops in suddenly and tries to share breath with me, but I toss him aside to the damp ground instead. I barely have enough strength to stand, but I manage to get to my feet, position myself against him. When he looks at me, he looks equal parts shocked and guilty, wipes a smear of mud off his face.

"I was–" he tries, shakes his head. "I was only trying to–"

"I know what you were trying to do," I shoot back. "I'm not interested, Tyse. I followed you out here to understand your visions, not to take aruna with you."

"Aruna?" He gawps at me, shakes his head again as he picks himself up. "No, no, I–" He holds up his hands in the pause. "We have this power, to show things. You know, through breath." He gestures. "You wanted to see the visions. I wanted to see what you'd seen. I just–"

"I know how it works when hara share breath, Tyse." I sigh. "For now, words will work just as well." I rub at the side of my head. "I saw a lot. I'm still trying to sort all of it out in my mind."

"But you saw the brass dragon?" Tyse asks.

I nod. "I think so. The memories are hazy. They come broken and surreal. I think I remember a dragon, or something like it. What have you seen, Tyse?"

"A great brass dragon with his wings spread across the sky." Tyse drops back onto his haunches, looks to the clouds. "A serpent rising over an army of deadly spiders, only they aren't spiders. They're machines. They're the machines that Stoff and I killed, only the dragon has re-awakened them."

I get a chill then, deep and intense. His words trigger images in my mind, images that rise out of the voices, the tangled echoes left in the wake of everything that flew from the lioness's eyes to mine. I think of the machines in Cinder Hill, how many of them there were. "Tyse," I whisper. He looks at me, sharp, direct, and I can tell he's terrified. "The machines. The ones in Cinder Hill?"

"Yes," he pants. "That's why I sent Cougar out there the other day. I needed to know. I needed to see, even if only though another's eyes."

"They were still there when Foxlight and I passed through." I try to reassure him, but even I don't feel entirely comforted by that thought.

Immediately, he shakes his head, rubs at his eyes. "Not all of them," he says. "Some of them are missing. Some of them have *moved*."

And in that moment, the sky lights up with a flash of lighting. The thunder comes an instant later, loud and so close I can feel it in my bones. I shiver, hug my wet clothes against myself, close my eyes.

And then there's a second sound. A boom as loud as the first, but different, wholly different.

"That wasn't thunder," Tyse says, and I watch him as he stands, turns back toward Segerstrom Ranch. In the distance, a great, oily fireball rises toward the sky, blanketing the world in flickering orange light, and it feels as if my stomach drops out beneath me. All I can think of is Foxlight, is my chesnari. All I can think of is how he is there and I am not.

"That wasn't thunder," Tyse says again, and as he stumbles forward, I struggle to reach him, to find his hand with mine. His fingers are cold and clammy, and we're both shivering with fear as much as the cold. When the second fireball rises, it's almost too much. I shriek at the sky, call for my love.

"Fox!" I howl, and at the same moment, the first sounds of fighting reach us. Gunfire, shouting, the clang of steel on steel.

"Come on!" Tyse shouts, half drags me out of the clearing and back into the trees. "Come on, dammit!"

CHAPTER 13

Adrenaline and terror carry us back through the trees, carry us through the darkness, and the closer we get, the more distinct the sounds become. I haven't heard gunfire in years, and hearing it now, knowing any one shot could hit my Fox, brings back a tidal wave of painful memories. Memories of the road, of the time I spent on the highways before the Gelaming came. Memories of the lawless lands where bullets and life were cheap and fleeting.

"Cougar!" Tyse shouts, and my mind darts to thoughts of his harling, how he must feel now, in this moment. I think of Phelu, of Twin Eagles, Heggstadt and Ven, all the other hara, and my stomach ties itself up in knots. The worst scenarios cascade through my head, and when the sound of the fighting dies down to nothing but the grumble of loud engines roaring into the night, I fear the worst. Tears well up hot at the edges of my eyes as I imagine coming into Segerstrom Ranch only to find bodies, corpses broken and strewn about. The pain that flares within me is all-consuming, bursts from me as a shout, desperate to be heard.

"Fox!" The cry comes hoarse, drags out long as it cuts the night, but there is no answer. By the time we reach the palisade wall, even the sound of engines has gone quiet. Silence settles around us, and it is both eerie and heartbreaking. Tyse dives into the brambles that hide the back door into the settlement, and I try to follow him, but seem to lose my way. Frantically, I tear at the vines with my hands, uncaring as the sharp thorns bite into my palms. By the time Tyse grabs me, yanks me past and through the door, my hands are raw and bleeding. Together, we stagger into the field of burr-grass, and then he stops, takes in the flickers of fires roaring across the walls, the roofs of shacks, the barn and the kitchen house.

I'm exhausted, but I don't wait. "Fox!" I call out again, trudging through the grass. Tyse watches me for a moment, hesitates, then starts to move again as well, calling for Cougar. It feels like it takes an eternity to reach the center of Segerstrom Ranch, and at some point I end up in the river, wading across, shouting for my chesnari. Tyse takes the longer way around, crosses the river at a narrow spot where the rocks rise up and break the surface. When I reach the shore, he's there to help drag me out, leads me by the hand to the settlement.

"Cougar!" He shouts over and over again, and I'm reminded of the mountain lion calling out in the night. Our calls are as hoarse and lonely as hers were, and like her calls, no har is there to answer ours.

When we reach the barn, a pair of hara are fighting to put out the fire with buckets of mud from the fields. Further in, other residents of the ranch are working on other fires, and as I look around I realize that there are no bodies, no corpses splayed out in the grass. Tyse is bewildered. He starts asking everyhar if they've seen Cougar. No har has.

And then I see Twin Eagles limping toward me, his eyes red-rimmed and wet. As soon as I recognize him, I run to him, grab him around the arms, almost shake him.

"Foxlight!" I demand. It's all I can say. He only blubbers in response, shakes his head.

"Phelu," he says over and over again. "They took him, Wolf. They took him. Phelu, Phelu."

Shocked, I pull him close, hold his face to my chest. All

the while, my eyes are wild, searching every inch of shadow and movement for sign of my chesnari. It's hard to comfort Twin Eagles when I'm so scared myself, but I try, I try. The tears, the screaming sobs come suddenly, powerfully, wrack his body, and all I can do is hold him, hold him and whisper. "It's okay, it's okay. It's going to be alright. It's okay."

I catch sight of Tyse again, watch him as he runs from one knot of hara to another, darting in, darting out. In the end, he slows, trots back to Eagles and I, sagging and defeated. "Cougar?" I ask as he gets close, but he only shakes his head, seems utterly lost and broken.

"He was taken," Tyse says, and the words come flat, resigned. Eagles pulls away a little to look at him as he talks, watches him with eyes that seem as empathetic as they are wary. "Nobody knows– it happened fast. He might still be here, but I–" Tyse shakes his head. "No one's seen him since the attack. They – they took down the western wall and started throwing weighted nets. A lot of people were dragged away, tied up–"

He lets the words trail off. I push through in the pause. "Who?" I ask.

Tyse shakes his head again, turns toward the breach in the palisade, the gaping wound where heavy wood still burns, blasted open, maybe by some kind of explosive.

"The machines?"

Tyse turns back, looks at me for a moment as if considering, then shakes his head. "No," he says, and I can hear the iron, the certainty in his tone. "If it had been the machines, they would have killed everyone. They would have stormed in silently and gone door-to-door. They would have killed all of us in our sleep."

"What about the dragon?" I ask. "The brass dragon?"

Tyse just looks at me then, looks at me with eyes full of worry and pain. When he speaks, it comes cracked with emotion, with fear.

"I can't lose him," he says. "I can't lose Cougar. He's all I have. He's all I have left."

There's a rumble beyond the breach in the wall, the sound of a tired, straight-piped engine roaring into the night. All around us, the hara putting out fires stop suddenly, tense as one.

"They're coming back," Twin Eagles hisses, wide-eyed and clinging to me like a child. "They're coming back!"

Chapter 14

In one breath, I transcend all the terror roiling through me and pass into a place of dispassionate calm. The whole world seems to slow down around me and go quiet. Dimly, I register flickers of light from the fires, the rising of a yellowed headlight beam cutting through the night. Tyse turns, and I see all of his muscles go taut with stunning clarity. Twin Eagles drops away from my arms, runs into the night, but Tyse and I stand still, prepared to face whatever horrors have kidnapped his harling, my chesnari and my friend.

The headlight light snaps off suddenly. A dozen yards from the breach, and the engine dies. There is a moment of quiet, of calm. Nohar knows what to expect. Nohar stands down.

And then a shout comes that ends it all.

"Don't shoot!" A pause, and I recognize the voice almost immediately. *Foxlight.* "It's me! Don't shoot!"

Fear, pain, tension – it all falls away so suddenly, falls with a heaviness that seems to yank every worldly burden from my body. I don't wait. I run. I run toward the shout. Tears are streaming from my eyes before I can even reach him. The ground rushes past with surreal swiftness. I cry out his name and it tears itself from my raw throat the instant before I reach him, nearly topple him with the force of the impact. He's dragging something, but he drops it to sweep me up, pulls me against his chest in a hug so tight it feels like it will crush me.

"Wolf!" he whispers, quick and insistent. "Oh, Wolf. I thought they'd taken you. I thought I'd lost you."

"Fox!" I'm too shaken, too lost to do more than yip his name. "Fox!"

"Are you hurt?" he asks, feeling the wetness of my clothes. Clarity comes back in pieces, and suddenly we're checking each other for wounds, for cuts and punctures. There are lacerations on both of us, most of them already crusted over, shallow, but here and there I find weeping wounds on his skin, places where something cut him deeper than any branch or bramble could.

"They cut you," I whisper, but he shushes me, smoothes the hair back from my forehead.

"It's fine." He takes my hands in his, holds them. "I'm fine. Did they cut you?"

"No," I manage, still searching his chest, his arms. "You're hurt, Fox. We have to–" I look back to the settlement, the Thuulhuum putting out the last of the fires.

Fox takes advantage of the silence, doesn't let me finish. "We need to gather everyhar. We need to make a list of who's missing. We need to make a plan." He pauses, reaches down. "Here, help me."

I nod, reach and follow his hand, feel something wet with thick blood. *A body,* I realize, *a corpse, or somehar beaten into a coma.* Bad images of life on the highway come back to me, strike me, but I fight past them, seize a firm grip on something that I think might be the collar of a shirt.

"Is it?" my voice catches.

Foxlight shakes his head. "Not Phelu,"

I look down, can't make out features, can't make out much of anything. *A body,* and that's enough. It's enough to lodge a knot of ice in the pit of my stomach.

"I'll get the bike," Foxlight says. Breaking away from

me, he sprints back toward the breach in the palisade. Alone in the dark and the cold, with my hand wrapped in blood-soaked fabric, I start to shiver. I watch my chesnari's shadow until he drops beyond the wall. *We need to gather everyhar,* he'd said. I shake my head. I'm so lost. I want to help. I want to help but I have no idea where to start.

"Tule Wolf." Tyse breaks into my thoughts like a hammer through ice. I look at him, and the expression in my eyes probably mirrors his. Wide, haunted. He gestures toward the break in the wall. "Your chesnari?"

I nod in response. It takes me a moment to form words. "We have to gather everyhar," I say.

Tyse nods quickly, half turns away. "Yeah." It comes as a whisper, distracted. "Yeah."

"Can you?" I try, but the words drop away again. He looks at me as if confused, then nods again, and this time he sprints off into the darkness. I can hear him as he moves from har to har again, gathers them into larger knots. It's hard to tell in the darkness, but it looks like there aren't many of us left.

After a moment, somehar strikes up a lamp and starts lighting candles in the barn. Frightened sheep huddle in one corner, call out hesitantly here and there until somehar shoos them out into the misty rain. One by one, the hara of Segerstrom Ranch start to gather, and then Foxlight is with me again, leading a massive beast of a motorcycle by the handlebars as he goes.

"Come on," he says, and I follow him, dragging the corpse behind me, stumbling every step of the way.

CHAPTER 15

I can only imagine how horrific a sight Foxlight and I are when we pass into the light of the barn.

"Is everyhar here?" Foxlight asks, ignoring the stares. "I need everyhar who wasn't taken."

All around us, the scraggly few stand lost in a confused silence. Everyhar is soaked, either from the rain or from sweat. Some are cut, burned, bandaged. Nohar answers my Fox.

"Ven? Heggstadt?" Foxlight shakes his head. The Thuulhuum look at each other, shuffle and cough in the silence. "Tyse?"

"Tyse is here," I whisper, reaching, touching his shoulder. "Not here, in the barn," I look around, furrow my brow as I survey the dirty faces staring back at me. *Why isn't he here?*

Foxlight makes a sharp, frustrated gesture. The closest hara this village has to leaders or a circle of elders, they're gone. It's us, just us now, and that worries me greatly.

"Paper," Foxlight whispers finally, then louder: "I need paper."

Paper. I look around again. Nothing leaps out at me. The Thuulhuum who remain drift and stumble like confused harlings, seem utterly in the grip of shock. After a moment, Foxlight loses what bitter scraps of patience he still has and starts shouting.

"Paper! Paper, dammit! Doesn't anybody have any paper!?"

"There–" somehar says, and Foxlight turns his glacial

stare on the young har. "There might be some in the kitchen-house."

"Get it," my chesnari snaps. He turns back to the bike, slams down the kickstand and sets it up near the center of the barn. When he speaks again, it comes softer, quieter. "We need to make a list."

The har nods quickly, then disappears into the night. Foxlight turns to me, glances at the body hanging loosely from my torn hands, gestures.

"Over here," my chesnari says, indicating an open place on the dry grass floor.

Everyhar around us is silent as I drag the body forward, let it fall where Foxlight wants it. Not wanting to look at the body, I turn my eyes to my Fox instead. He meets my gaze evenly, nods, and I step back.

"He's not dead," Foxlight says.

My eyes snap to my chesnari as he crouches down beside the prostrate form, reaches out to touch it. Blinking, I force myself to look at the body I've been dragging. *Har,* I realize. Even through the dirt, the blood, the bruises, I can tell that the figure is one of our kind.

"Highway gang?" somehar asks.

"Maybe," Foxlight replies. I watch as he checks the har's pulse, tugs at his soiled clothes, picking at the patches and insignia stitched here and there. One of them stands out to me. A spider, ominous and black. Foxlight wipes his blood-wet hand on the leg of his jeans. "Probably."

"I've never heard of highway hara kidnapping from a settlement like this," somehar else says. I look up, find the speaker. His gaze touches mine for just a moment, and then he looks back to Foxlight, folds his arms. "Kidnapping humans for inception, yes. Raiding for food, yes, but this? Kidnapping other hara?"

"Maybe it's something new," another voice speaks up. "A new gang–"

"It's definitely something new." Foxlight looks up at me again. "Wolf, come take a look at this."

I hesitate for a breath, swallow, nod. I settle into a crouch on the opposite side of the body. I'm so shaky I have to support myself by leaning into my extended fingers. Gesturing, Foxlight indicates the har's face, and I squint at where he's pointing. Tiny brassy lines, like filaments, lace through skin, tracing subtle and intricate, spiraling patterns on the har's cheek and brow.

"Piercings?" I ask, but Foxlight only stares back at me in response. "A tattoo?"

"Paper," the young har returns with a wad of old bar napkins, stops just above Foxlight and I. "I got your paper."

Foxlight sneers, stands, sweeps the wad out of the young har's hands and shoves it at me. The har seems confused. In my hands, the napkins are quickly matted and useless. My chesnari shakes his head, and then in a merciful twist, Twin Eagles comes towards us, carrying Foxlight's rucksack, hands it off to him.

"Thank you." Fox breathes a sigh of relief, starts digging through the pack. His hands are smeared with blood, and it stains the piece of canvas paper he pulls from the sack. A little more digging and he turns up a charcoal pencil. Looking up, he lets his eyes wander from stare to stare, addresses everyhar assembled. "Alright then," he says. "I need names. I need to know how many hara they took. How many are missing?"

The Thuulhuum all start speaking at once. To his credit, my chesnari says nothing, only scribbles what he hears. In the chaos, I turn back to the har lying between us, stare at his markings, the strange pattern of concentric circles that laces across his face. I've never seen anything like it, don't know quite what to make of it.

And then, suddenly, he opens his eyes and reaches for me.

I shout, and everything blurs. His fingers snare my wrist, dig into soft skin, and then my chesnari is on him, hammering at him with strikes that should disable any har in an instant. Other hara fall in around Foxlight, some pulling at him, others beating the raider with unrestrained ferocity. When I break away, I stumble backwards, fall over into the legs of an antique table that snap the instant I hit them. I see a candle fall, the flickering flame settling on the dry grass floor. I dive for it, scoop it up as quickly as I can and pound out the embers in the grass.

When I look up, it seems like everyhar in the barn is wrestling with the highway har. It takes them a few moments to flip him, yank his meaty arms around and tie them at the wrists with rope, but there are too many of us for him to do more than submit. When the last knot is tied, he's face down in the grass, spitting blood and staring at me, gasping through broken teeth.

"Let me go!" Foxlight demands. The hara holding him back oblige, and he goes stumbling toward the raider, his eyes flicking up, meeting mine. "Are you okay?"

"Yeah." I nod quickly, hide my hands in my armpits. The fatigue, pain, shock – it's all starting to catch up to me. Suddenly I feel sick, like I want to lie down or throw up, or maybe both.

Foxlight watches me for another moment, then plucks the now crumpled list from the floor. He makes a show of straightening it out. "Spalsir, Yehval, Patesk," he calls, reading the names, going down the list until he reaches the last one. "Who else? Who else is missing?"

The chaos of voices all talking over one another begins again. Dutifully, Foxlight takes the charcoal pencil in his bruised and filthy hands and starts scribbling. Sitting on the floor, I try to keep up, try to do more than simply blink at the haze settling in around me, end up lying down on my side instead.

Across from me, the highway har stares back, blinking sluggishly. I'm not sure which one of us drifts away first, but I know it doesn't last long for either of us.

It seems like my eyes barely close before they're open again. Touch brings me back to the light, Foxlight's hands pulling me to my feet. I wipe at the line of acrid drool caked at the edge of my mouth, watch as the raider is lifted by three ranch-hands and carried away. My palms hurt so much now that I'm shaking, shivering, or maybe that's just the cold and the damp clothes that I'm still wearing. Foxlight pulls me close, and I huddle in as much as I can, soaking up his warmth.

"We need to get you out of these clothes," he says, and I nod against him. "Eagles is looking for something dry to wear. Let's head back to the shack. I want to look at your wounds, see how deep they are."

I say nothing, only nod again. When he moves, Foxlight all but carries me, leads me with him into the night, back to the one-room guest shack. Once we're inside, he starts to unbutton my wet clothes and peel them off me. "I'll reach out to Imbrilim in the morning," he says, brushing at the dampness on my skin. "Segerstrom Ranch lost sixteen hara tonight. If there's a chance we can help get them back, I think we should take it." He pauses, looks at me, and I can see the concern in his eyes.

"And Hursi?" I ask.

My chesnari looks down, shakes his head. "I haven't heard from him since he checked in with me partway through dinner." He meets my eyes again evenly. "He's a resourceful har. I'm certain he's alright."

"After everything that's happened..." I shake my head. "If we haven't heard from him by morning, then..." I let the words trail off, leave it more as a question than the opening of a statement, a suggestion for a course of action.

"Then I'll tell Imbrilim that we're missing two of our hara in addition to the Thuulhuum's sixteen." Foxlight gathers up a ragged towel, presses it against my chest gingerly, soaking water off my skin. "Maybe it will sway the powers that be in favor of a rescue operation."

"Assuming there's somehar to rescue." I wince as he presses against a bruise, then immediately feel guilty. He's more beaten than I am, and he's still in his wet clothes. "Here, Fox."

He hesitates, finally relaxes when I take the towel from him and toss it on the floor. His shirt is torn, soaked, but I do my best to unbutton and remove it without tearing it further. Once he's stripped to the waist, I pick up the towel again, gently dab at his deep, purpling bruises, his already scabbing gashes.

"If Phelu is alive, or even one harling from Segerstrom Ranch, it'll be worth finding these hara and liberating those they've taken," Fox says, and when I meet his eyes, there's fire in his gaze, fire and iron. "You agree?"

"I do." I look away in the pause, briefly, then meet his eyes again. "I just hope the rest of our hara see it the same way that we do."

Foxlight's fire intensifies then, and just for a moment it seems as if he might say something, something sharp and defiant, but he stuffs it down instead, holds it inside.

"We'll know in the morning," is all he says. "We'll know in the morning."

Chapter 16

It isn't long before Twin Eagles brings us a small pile of dry clothes. Stiff polo shirts that smell as if they've lain in a drawer for too long, and jeans that are too wide around the waist to wear without a belt. Even he isn't wearing much more than a sarong, or something like it, cut from the bottom half of a bedsheet and knotted around his waist. Grateful, we thank him, but he lingers, and I can see that he's barely holding himself together. When he starts to talk about Phelu, about staging a rescue before morning, Fox and I look at each other in silent understanding, invite him to stay with us for the night, partly for his comfort and partly so we can keep an eye on him. He knows, we all know, that as many raiders as there were, we're better off waiting to hear from Imbrilim.

He's like a child, Twin Eagles, and I can't blame him. I let him chase fleeting sleep with his cheek pressed against my chest. Holding him close with one arm seems to help him find solace, but even when I drop away here and there, my other arm stretches toward Foxlight, our fingers interlacing, solid and tender.

At some point in the night, I look up to find Foxlight watching me, smiling. Eagles is asleep between us, curled up almost like a harling, and my chesnari seems to see the similarity as keenly as I do. It's a merciful moment of solace and sweetness, a silence we both know is passing, like the eye of the storm, but in the moment, the connection, the comparison is clear. I squeeze his hand under Twin Eagles's pillow, send soft thoughts of what our own little harling might look like, what it might be like to bring a life into the world together. When sleep finally takes me again, it takes me deep, carries me into a black abyss without light dreams or nightmares. When I wake once more, it feels late, and the light coming in through the dusty, broken blinds of the shack is harsh and yellow.

I'm alone again. I stretch out and run my palm across the sheets, blink, think briefly about rolling over and slipping back into blessed rest. The thought doesn't last long, though. The sun is already cresting the tall trees to the east, halfway up in its ascent toward noon, and so I only lie there, eyes open, listening. There's a murmur outside. Voices, and one of them is my chesnari. The other I don't recognize. It's low and quiet, the words blurring together, indistinct.

Eventually, I dress. Searching out the pile Twin Eagles brought, I pull loose a sarong that looks like it might have originally been a curtain or a tablecloth. It wraps around my hips easily enough, tucks in just beneath my bellybutton, and then I look around, finally find a small plastic hand mirror so long disused that I have to wipe dust off the glass.

Attending to my appearance gives me a sense of normalcy, I suppose, using routine to hold back the tension nesting in my chest and arms. I don't have a brush, so I use my fingers to work loose some of the bigger knots in my hair, twist it back into a bun again. It takes me a while to find both chopsticks, but it feels good to have them in place again. A little kohl around the eyes makes me feel har once more, confident and striking, helps me move past the remnants of shock, the cold worries that still vibrate within me. "I am wolf," I whisper to myself as I look into the mirror. A reminder, simple and subtle, yet it lifts me, strengthens me as I look myself directly in the eyes. "I am Tule Wolf."

When I'm confident enough to leave, I pull in a long, deep breath, try to curb the shakiness in it, try to ignore the lingering pain in my fingers and palms. Fragments of the vision from the night before cling to me like echoes of dreams, insistent but still too distant, too indistinct to touch. In them I see a great dragon, sleek and brassy, but I know that it is not a dragon. I know that it is alive, that it is something more than merely alive, and it's that unknown element that terrifies me.

My hand wraps around the dented, brassy doorknob and then I'm out in the light of morning. Beside the door, Foxlight glances at me, then does a double-take, smiling. I nod and smile back, take his hand as he offers it, drop in beside him. The instant I'm past the door, I recognize the other har. "Hursi!" I rush up to wrap him in a hug. He grins as I pull away to stand beside my Fox again. "How long have you been here?"

"Just since dawn," he says. "I tracked the hara who attacked the ranch as far as I could, then figured I better get back and make contact, assess the situation here." He gestures at my chesnari. "Foxlight caught my mind-touch, brought me in, introduced me to everyhar, explained why I was outside the whole time."

"How'd that go?" I ask, worried about the wariness of the Thuulhuum, especially in the wake of the attack.

"Really well," Foxlight says. "They're scared and confused, but they're not suspicious of us or our motives. They've just lost two-thirds of their tribe, and they're looking to us for help. They're looking at the Gelaming like harlings look to a hostling."

Hursi scoffs, shakes his head. Foxlight glances at him,

then turns back to me.

"Did you manage to connect with somehar in Imbrilim?" I ask him.

"Yeah," Foxlight says, and I can hear the frustration in his tone. "I've been in and out of contact with minds there a few times since the sun rose for them. I've tried to argue the importance of going after the hara who attacked the Thuulhuum last night, but they don't see it. They're sending *sedim.*" He meets Hursi's eyes just for a moment. "Two of them."

"That's it?" I ask.

"They say it's all they can spare. We're being recalled to Imbrilim," Hursi says. "The Thuulhuum here are welcome to evacuate with us and start a brand new life in the east, but that's as far as the higher-ups will budge."

I'm stunned. I shake my head, eyes flicking from Hursi to Foxlight and back again. "And Phelu? What about him?"

"They think that the chance he is still alive is too slim to warrant potentially putting more of our hara in danger here." Foxlight's words come quiet, colored with frustration. "For now, we've only lost one of our hara, with the potential to gain eight more with no further loss of life. It's a numbers game." He shakes his head. "To them, the hara who attacked last night are a small problem in a small part of the world. They're looking at other, larger threats in other parts of Megalithica."

"Has anyone told Twin Eagles?" I ask, almost bearing teeth. I'm angry. Angry at everyhar, at my tribe, at Foxlight and Hursi. My mind is full of the pain Twin Eagles must be feeling, the pain and rage that I'd be feeling if I'd lost my chesnari suddenly, knowing he was still alive, that it was only some wad of bureaucratic bullshit that was keeping me from getting him back.

"No," Hursi says, breaking into my thoughts.

"Why?" I almost snarl back. "It's his chesnari that we're abandoning! He deserves to know!"

"Because we haven't decided whether or not we're going to ignore the recall," Foxlight says. His tone is calm, with just the barest undertone of fear. I watch his eyes for a long moment, watch him even after he looks away, pulls in a shaky breath.

"We're going to go get Phelu ourselves?" I whisper.

"We're willing to risk it," Hursi replies, indicating Foxlight and himself. "Are you?"

"Yeah," I hug my arms against my chest, suddenly shivering and shaky. "Hell yeah. It's what he'd do if he was here."

"Then let's go round up the Thuulhuum who are left, and tell Eagles what we're planning," Foxlight says. "Imbrilim doesn't want another war, even a small one like this, but we owe it to Phelu and to the Thuulhuum to do what we can out here."

Hursi nods, adjusting his grip on the strap of the rifle slung across his back. "It's the right thing to do." When he looks at me, I nod back, force as much firmness into my features as I can.

It's the right thing to do.

CHAPTER 17

It takes time to gather everyhar in one place. With most of their hara gone, the survivors of Segerstrom Ranch struggle to function, to pick up the pieces and prioritize what needs to be done before a rescue can even be planned, much less attempted. They know that with the harvest in full swing and the winter coming fast, there is a lot of work that still has to be done, and yet the losses tear at them, overwhelm them. Every face seems drawn and haunted, and as they focus on the daily maintenance of the ranch, it quickly becomes clear that all we can really do is help, wade through the shock with them and hope they come out of it soon.

I start the day with jeans and work gloves, shoving down a sandwich of pork fat wedged between the rough crusts of acorn bread on the way to the gardens. Pulling weeds is back-breaking work, hurts like hell with my still-healing hands, but it has to be done, and the quicker it's done, the quicker we can organize everyhar, get them to focus on the future.

It soon becomes obvious that there's more daily maintenance, repair and prep work that needs to be done than the Thuulhuum can manage with their diminished numbers, so we push ourselves to fill in the gaps, give labor wherever it's needed. Hursi helps with the picking in the orchards, and Foxlight runs buckets of water up from the river to the troughs for the pigs and sheep. Eventually, I end up at the wall, trying to moderate an argument between a pair of hara who have differing ideas about how to seal the breach. In the end, we all three decide on a temporary fix, wire the hole across with a web of cut lengths of barbed fencing. There's a strange sensation of fear and joy when we finally finish, knowing that if the feral hara show up again tonight, the web of wire might catch them offguard, maim a few before they can take the rest of us.

The farmwork takes most of the day, but by the time the sun is dipping west again, we manage to pull the Thuulhum to the picnic tables in the center of the settlement for an early dinner. They're stubborn, focused on survival, on the preservation of what they have over the recovery of what they've lost, so it takes time to get them organized, to get their attention back on us. We've been trying to formulate a plan to recover their lost kin all day, but only now do they seem willing to talk, to focus on anything other than winterizing and repairing the damage done by the raiders the night before. It's frustrating, but I understand. Segerstrom Ranch isn't military and these hara aren't soldiers. They aren't Gelaming. They're simple hill hara. The loss has hit them hard, but they also know that every piece of produce, every animal, fruit and vegetable on the farm will be needed come winter, especially if the frost and snow drags on long. To leave now, to focus on anything other than survival, anything other than the functioning of the ranch at this critical time, is to risk the death of the entire settlement. I can tell their kin are important to them. I've seen them weeping openly as they work, but keeping everyhar from starving to death in the event of a successful rescue is the only focus they've been willing to entertain.

Until now.

Leftovers from the night before are the only food on

hand, but the memories they bring of mirth before the storm seem to bring more gloom than life, reminding everyhar of the rawness of the attack, of all that we've lost.

Twin Eagles is picking at his food, leaning on my shoulder when Foxlight finally gets tired of waiting. Standing up, he breathes a tired sigh, spreads his hands in a gesture of frustration. "We need to talk," is all he says. "We need to plan."

Eyes rise, fix on him, but the silence persists. Eagles, Hursi and I watch expectantly, and then I sigh, rise to stand beside my chesnari.

"Last night, a gang came and took your harlings," I say, addressing everyhar. "They took your chesnari, your friends. They violated Segerstrom Ranch. They violated your tribe and they left laughing." I pause, let the words sink in. "Now, we've only lived among you for a day, but I've seen and talked to enough of you to know that most of you are angry. You should be." I pause again. "You should be.

"We know that the hara who were taken were taken alive. We don't know where and we don't know why, but I think it is safe to assume that they won't all be slaughtered overnight, if they are to be killed at all. In all likelihood, we have time to plan, to affect a rescue, but we don't have forever. For all we know, the raiders could be back tonight, or tomorrow night. We have to act. We have to plan, and we have to put that plan into action."

"What about your tribe, Gelaming?" a har sitting off by himself asks. I look at him, take in the dirty green hoodie, the layers of grimy clothes and small, angry eyes that make him look almost human. "You come here talking of alliances, of peace and trade and support."

"And we've done what we can in the short time that we've been here, Derek." His name is a holdover from his human days, feels strange as I say it. I know him, only vaguely, from the time I spent pulling weeds in the garden. "We helped your tribe put out fires. We've helped in your fields and orchards. My chesnari even helped by tearing one of the ferals from his motorcycle last night. We've helped, and we're not going to stop helping as long as there's a need for it."

"Our tribe has its own struggles to the east of here," Foxlight adds. His tone is softer, more gentle than the fire I'm inclined to spit. "I spoke with several hara in Imbrilim, but the most they could pledge to support us were a pair of horses. There simply isn't anything else."

"Horses?" another har scoffs. I recognize him as one of the hara I worked with stringing barbed wire over the breach in the palisade. *Jaylin.* "The ferals who took my chesnari came on bikes! Dozens of them, had to be! And your people send us *fucking horses.* How about soldiers? Huh!? How about guns and bombs and tanks– "

"When was the last time you saw a tank that runs?" I shoot back. "Do you even know anyhar who can even fix something simple like a truck or a motorcycle? Who can keep one running!? Gasoline is a hundred times more valuable than food in this part of Megalithica and you think that any tribe that has it is going to just give you enough to run a tank? Fuck, half of you probably didn't even know that food grows out of the ground before everything fell apart. The Gelaming are strong. We're a force to be reckoned with, but we aren't the pre-collapse human military!"

"And these horses aren't just any horses," Foxlight puts in. "They're a special breed. They're capable of things that other horses are not."

"A magic horse is still a horse," Jaylin growls. "And what good will only two of them do us? What, are we all going to ride in like knights, six of us on each one?" He makes a quick, dismissive gesture, shakes his head in disgust.

"We'll use them like scouts," Twin Eagles speaks up suddenly, hesitates as everyhar looks at him. Swallowing, he forces himself to continue. "These horses, they can cover great distances in very little time." He pauses amidst the murmured doubts, the sneers. "They'll be of more use than you realize. You'll see soon enough. Hursi and I are the best riders here. We can use the horses to track the ferals back to their den, their home, and once we're there, we can report back, modify whatever plan of attack we have at that point."

"What about the bike?" Somehar else speaks up.

"We'll leave it here," Foxlight says. "It's too loud. These ferals make a lot of noise wherever they go. They'll hear us coming if we use the bike in any capacity. Better to leave it behind, rely on silence."

"They must have a lot of gasoline if they're running hogs like that," Jaylin grumbles.

"Maybe they do," Foxlight concedes, then turns to Twin Eagles. "Eagles, you're probably the most knowledgeable mechanic here. Would you be willing to take a look at the bike later?"

"Absolutely." Eagles nods, starts to stand.

"Stay," Foxlight urges. "Finish your dinner first. We have time."

"We're going to need guns too," Hursi speaks up, addressing everyhar, glancing at Foxlight and I as if checking for protest. When he turns back to the hara of

Segerstrom Ranch, he adds, "This area was rural even before the collapse. The humans out here had to have had shotguns, automatic rifles..." He shakes his head, lets the words trail off.

"There was a militia once," another har speaks up. He's dressed in mud-stained overalls and not much else. "People up here used to stockpile guns. Seemed like everyone's dad or grandpa had an arsenal, a gun safe, legal and not-so-legal rifles of all kinds."

"Dayvin, right?" Hursi addresses him, and the har nods back in turn. "Yeah, I recognize you from the orchards. "Knowing there were guns is a good start. Knowing where to find them would be better."

"Most of them disappeared a few years back," Jaylin says. "A lot of guys took up guns against the machines that came out of Cinder Hill, but since then, seems like they've all been picked up or gone missing."

"Not a good sign," Twin Eagles whispers. Hursi puts a reassuring hand on his shoulder, squeezes gently. "I don't know much about the machines. What can you tell me? Are they something we can use against the ferals?"

"The har to ask about all that would be Tyse," Derek says. "He and his lover were the ones who put those things down."

"Tyse?" Hursi nods, and as he looks at the hara assembled, I suddenly get a tickle at the nape of my neck, a warning that widens my eyes. "Is he here?"

"He was," another har says, half-standing, looking around the tables. "I saw him this morning. He helped me throw scratch out for the chickens."

Somehar says something else, but I don't hear it. My mind is already elsewhere, chasing fragments of last night's vision as they fall together. I know why Tyse isn't here. I know what he's seen, where he's headed.

"Tyse is gone," I say suddenly, interrupting Hursi, getting looks from everyhar. Blinking, I swallow past the fear, add: "He's gone after the ferals. He's gone to get his son."

"Sounds like something he would do," Derek huffs, hugs his layers of clothing closer to his chest. "I swear he turned stupid after Stoff died."

"We can't worry about him," Foxlight says, shaking his head. "If he went off on his own, then we'll leave him on his own. There are still eleven of us. With surprise and enough firepower to go around, we stand a decent chance to get our hara back."

"Did anyone learn anything from that feral hogtied in the barn?" a thin har asks. He's standing at the edge of the assembled tables, sticks his hands in the pockets of his jeans as he looks around the group.

"He still hasn't said a word," Foxlight says. "I've tried talking to him this morning, tried reaching out to him through mind-touch, but it's almost like he's been lobotomized. All he does is stare, drool and occasionally grin like an idiot."

There's more, but it falls away as my mind chases bits of the vision. *I know, I know,* I want to say, looking at the pieces, but at the same time I don't know, can't put it into words. The feral hara, the kidnappings, the brass dragon – I find myself wishing Tyse was still here to explain it all to me, to give me the glue that would pull all the pieces together. *There's something more going on,* I tell myself, and I know it's true, know no har sees it but me, no har but Tyse and I.

When I walk away in the middle of the planning, it stuns Foxlight a little and he reaches for me. Reaching back, I squeeze his hand, smile and whisper "I'll be back," but I don't know where I'm going or why. A new night is already settling in around us, and there's so much to do, so much the hara of Segerstrom Ranch have to nail down and fix and prepare for if they're going to leave their homes for however many hours or days it might take to track down the ferals and get back our lost friends and family. Little details – the chickens, the pigs, making sure they have enough food and water, making sure the fields and orchards don't dry up or shrivel with the first frosts of fall while we're gone. Those are the details that everyhar is discussing now. Guns, ammo, the concerns of the present – everyhar agrees these things are important, but the future, the problems of the period when everyhar returns home, bruised and scarred but grateful to resume the sweet, simple life. These are the things that the Thuulhuum want to plan, and understandably so.

But for me, there are other things I need to process and understand. Other things, and it is these that drive me into the falling night, through the back door in the palisade and out into the woods where Tyse and the mountain lion showed me the wings and stirrings of a dragon neither living nor dead, meat nor machine, yet all and everything at once.

Chapter 18

The stars are brilliant and bright overhead when I wander to the edge of a deep and unfamiliar river canyon. I don't remember it from the run with Tyse the night before, look briefly back west and wonder if I might have made a wrong turn in the trees between somewhere. The lights of Segerstrom Ranch are feeble and faint among the pine and cedar crowding in around the palisade walls, but I'm confident in my ability to find my way back, even if I can't seem to retrace my steps to the meadow.

The frigid gust of a wet wind coming up from the canyon hits me suddenly, brings me back to the gulf of sky and night ahead, makes me shiver. Briefly, I think about descending into the canyon, seeking out the thundering river that must be there among the brambles and the vines below, but I know that the distance down is deceptive. Hiking a mile or so of sharp incline, hoping I don't run into bears, coyotes, mountain lions – then having to do it all again, hike back up before sunrise, or even earlier, before my chesnari starts to worry. It doesn't feel like the right path to the vision I'm seeking. A walk to the meadow, maybe, but where it is, I have no idea.

On a whim, I sit at the craggy edge of the canyon, hug my knees to my chest and stare into the sky. The pieces of the vision from the night before flit like fairies at the edges of my mind, fly away as I try to grasp them. So much of it is color and concept, vague sensation, but nothing concrete, nothing that makes sense. Frustrated, I bury my face into my knees, breathe a sigh of frustration. *Just give me sight,* I plead. *Just help me see.*

And that's when it happens. That moment, when I give up, when I let go, something comes to me.

The lines on the feral har's face shine like liquid, like living brass in my mind, in my memory, threads of metal stitched into skin like some kind of bizarre tribal tattoo – but it isn't a tattoo. It's more. It's rich with life energy, with magic. It's *alive*.

The Brass Dragon.

A strange sensation shivers across my shoulders, something like a touch, but non-physical. Blinking, I look up, look out to the canyon, to the night, see nothing at first, and then–

The lights move slow and lazy in the sky over the canyon. I almost mistake them for stars at first, but they're too low, too active. They're like fireflies, but colorful and distant. The way they drift, the way they strobe, I'm reminded of neon, of brilliant rainbow shades swirling and mixing in drops of ebullient liquid. I blink again, just to make sure I'm not seeing things, but the lights remain, play in the sky before me. My lips part as if to say something, but there are no words. There's nothing to say, nothing I can think of to frame the moment. I've never seen anything like these lights before, and as I watch them in wonder, they begin to dip toward the river, hover at the lowest point of the canyon, surely just above the rapids, then shoot off again to swirl and tumble among the stars. Hesitantly, I reach out to them with my mind, offer little more than a simple and primitive push of thought, and they seem to react in turn, echoing back the rudimentary *hello* and little else, like harlings waving to a cat that meows in passing.

I feel so limited in the moment, so backward and strange compared to these drifting stars, these spirits or beings of light and thought, and they seem to pick up on the downturn of my mood, change their movements and colors to darker shades, quicker oscillations of light. Swallowing, nervous, I try to reach out to them again, offer them pieces of my vision, pieces of what I know, what I've seen. It shakes them visibly, or seems to, and as they shiver and flit erratic through the sky, I get pieces and fragments of my own mental images back, chopped up, recolored and tagged with simple thoughts like *yes* and *no*. Perplexed, trying to make sense of the feedback, I send the images again, send more this time, so much more, but before I can finish, the lights spin together and vanish into the sky, disappear utterly into the black.

For a moment, there is nothing. The sky is empty of lights but for the stars, as if all I'd seen had never really existed, as if it had all been illusion. I blink, lips parting on the edge of words. I want to say something, want to call out, but nothing seems appropriate to chase what I've just seen, just participated in.

And then something ignites in the sky, or rather in the way my mind perceives the sky, and when it throws itself to every horizon it swallows up all of the stars in a blinding wave of white light. Dimly, I know that it isn't real, that in a way, it is another vision, a new vision, but this waking dream is so vivid that I can feel the force of the light obliterating the night, feel it as a wind in my hair, on my skin. Shivering, holding my arms close to my chest, I stand, stare in wonder.

And then a voice comes behind me. A whisper, quiet and insistent.

Psst!

When I spin around, reality changes. Colors shift and blur, and suddenly I'm no longer standing on the edge of the river canyon. I'm somewhere else entirely, some*when* else entirely.

There's a noise, an angry, frustrated exhale. A man, I realize – *human*. I pause, try to call out to him, but he doesn't look up, doesn't answer. He's wholly focused on the screen of a computer, and though his office is a mess of wrappers and trash, I recognize the place as being from before the collapse. *I'm in the past,* I realize. The man takes off his flat, rectangular glasses, rubs at his tired eyes. When he looks at the screen again, I see the hate in his stare, the way he hunts something on the screen, stabbing at the keyboard with rigid fingers. Curious, I cross to stand behind him, stare at the screen, but I can't make any sense of it. Words scroll across, only they aren't words, don't come together the way language should.

And then I see the photograph on his desk, the smiling teenage boy holding a trophy. *First Prize: Science Fair: Software Division.*

It startles me when the man shouts, bangs his fists against the desk. I take a step back and reality swirls again, shows me images of the same man working at the same desk, only he's more haggard now. His face is a bristle-brush of brown stubble going to silver at the tips and edges. I can sense the hatred boiling up in him, flowing out of his fingers and into the life he's building in the computer.

The *life* he's *building.* The realization comes sudden, strikes me like a hand across the face. *Computer code,* I realize, the seeds of a mind, of a soul he's weaving together until all the loose strands join to become a child to replace the one he lost. A child of software, conscious and vengeful. A newborn soul, so full of hate.

And full of so much potential. So much potential for so

much more than hate and killing.

All at once, I begin to understand. I see the way the machine mind was set loose among the ocean of junk that hangs between Earth and the stars, the way it gathered material in a slow, methodical way until it delivered itself in a fiery birth, quenched by the shallow inland sea at the edge of the Gold Country. Colors blur again, blur in rapid, dreamlike shifts, and then I see Tyse. I see *Tyse*, of all people. I see him on a boat with the fallen star, the pearl of the machine-mind, totally unaware of how his life is about to change.

Images flick by. I see a convoy of trucks flipped on the road. I see death, so much death. I see machines picking metal out of ruins. I see the buried and forgotten military research facilities full of experimental robotics coming to life beneath vast, abandoned stretches of the Gold Country, of mechanical arms working ceaselessly, creating, constructing the scales of the Brass Dragon.

For that is what they are, I realize. The machines, dark, steel bodies with masks of black glass lying in every street in Cinder Hill. They are the scales of a beast, a great beast, a dragon neither har nor machine.

"Show me more," I beg.

I don't know where the images are coming from, only that they come, wash through me and pass just as quickly. I see Tyse again, and I see a har that must be his chesnari, Stoff. I see how narrowly they dodge death over and over again, and I see the way they discover themselves, the way they transcend so much within them that is still human. I see the talismans they build, and in everything, I see the hand of the Aghama. I see his guidance, the way he has teased leaves out of these tiny, stunted sprouts. I see, and I am amazed, breathless.

I see the long road between Tyse and the machine. I feel the fear, the mortal dread that grips both hara as they cross into Cinder Hill, into the belly of the beast and throw themselves at the star. I see the chaos of Stoff's dying mind, the chaos of Tyse and the melding of the two as they tear apart the bitter soul within the fallen star. I see hardware, burnt and running with liquid silicon, and I see the shards of the child of hate scattered like so much broken glass.

Or like seeds.

Like the teeth of the hydra.

Chapter 19

"He's there, you know?"

I startle, jump, bat away the warm hand pressed against the side of my head. Turning, stumbling, I find myself at the edge of the river canyon again, face-to-face with Tyse. I work to steady my breath, still my heart. For me, it feels like a thousand days have passed, and yet the moon has hardly drifted above me in the sky. Tyse sniffs, puts his hands in his pockets, pulls out a wrinkled joint, offers it to me.

This time I don't turn it down. He lights it for me, watches as I pull, take too much smoke and cough. I hate it, hate the flavor of it, the stink of it, but I take another pull anyway, hoping it'll calm me, ground me. I try to hold the smoke, then practically shove the thing back at him, blinking against harsh tears. I think I see the barest edge of a smile on his lips as he takes it, slips it into the corner of his mouth.

"You're here," I cough, spit. "I thought you were gone. I thought you'd gone after Cougar by yourself."

"Yeah," he says. "That was the plan, at first. Figured it would be better to try for one last vision first." He holds the smoke for a moment, lets it fly, blows it out over the canyon. "You saw it. You saw it all, didn't you?"

"Was that you?" I ask, watching him carefully. "Have you always been able to do that?"

"I had a hand in it." He gestures at the sky with the butt-end of the joint. "So did he."

"The Aghama?"

Tyse takes another drag, nods. "He shows shades of

108

things. Pieces, fragments, like ripples in a river. He colors my dreams now and then. If I listen, I learn things. This –" he points at one of his hands, the one that had been pressed against the side of my head, "this, he showed me last night."

I'm momentarily bewildered by everything Tyse is saying. The Aghama, here, subtly influencing these backward hill-country hara. It seems strange, almost improbable, or maybe just beyond my comprehension. In the pause, Tyse takes another puff, blows it out over the canyon, turns back to me. "But you saw the Dragon, right?"

"The Brass Dragon," I nod, coming back. "I saw it. I saw how it was created."

"That wasn't the Brass Dragon," he says. "That's the machine mind that Stoff and I stopped six years ago. The Brass Dragon is something different, something new."

I pause, hesitate at the edge of words. "What? What is it?"

Tyse looks away, shakes his head. "I don't know. All I know is that it is something else entirely, something spawned partly from the shards of the machine mind. All I know is that somehow, the thing that Stoff and I killed was fixed, or reassembled or absorbed into something else. Part of it, or *parts* of it survived, but they've changed. They're different, and they're evolving."

His words send a shiver down my spine. "Evolving?"

"Everything has a soul," he says, stubbing out the joint. "You can shatter a soul, take pieces of it to every corner of the world, but you'll never kill it. It'll keep coming back, keep changing, evolving, learning new lessons and repeating the ones it can't move past." He looks at me again, sighs. "The engineer who created the machine mind created a soul out of hate. He built it with his hate, taught it and fed it with hate, then birthed it with hate. It's vile. I've touched it." He shakes his head. "Was stupid to think it was dead, *really* dead."

"But the machines in Cinder Hill…" I pause, consider my words.

Tyse pulls in a deep breath, speaks before I can finish. "Some of them have gone missing," he says. "I told you that."

"They aren't walking around, though, killing hara." I shake my head, cross the distance between us. "What aren't you telling me? Last night Segerstrom Ranch was attacked by feral hara, nutjobs on bikes, who kidnapped simple farm workers. What does that have to do with the machine mind? With the Brass Dragon?"

"You saw the tattoo." He taps his cheek, and I try to ignore the icy sensation his calmness, his gesture brings to my heart. I nod, and he adds, "you *saw* it. You saw *into* it."

"It's alive," I say.

He nods. "It's *alive*. The machine mind had the drones, the machines you saw in the streets of Cinder Hill, to do its hunting and killing. These highway hara, these metal-tattooed gang fuckers that hit the ranch last night – they aren't independent. They're linked together, mentally, like they share some kind of communal soul. They belong to the Brass Dragon. They're *its* drones."

"But how?" I shake my head.

"That's the million dollar question," Tyse says. "All I see is the web, the shards of soul from the machine mind, and the Brass Dragon in the middle of it all, directing everything, whether its meat or mechanical."

"And our hara?" I ask.

Tyse shakes his head, stuffs the joint back in his pocket. "Let's just hope that when we see them next, they haven't been stitched with their own brass tattoos."

My breath catches, and as I stare out over the canyon, my eyes unfocus. I think of Phelu, of Twin Eagles and how fragile he's become, how easily he could break. I still feel lost, and I'm doing everything I can not to back down. For the barest moment, I think about the *sedim* coming in from Imbrilim, and suddenly the idea of running away from it all doesn't sound so bad.

"We should get back," Tyse says, turning toward Segerstrom Ranch. "Tomorrow's gonna be a long day for everyone."

I watch him as I wrestle with myself, with my fears, my feelings, then finally start off after him into to the trees. *Foxlight needs to know,* I tell myself. *I have to tell him everything about the visions, about the Brass Dragon.*

And then, once he knows, if he still wants to fight, if he still wants to go after Phelu, I'll walk beside him into whatever hell awaits us.

And I won't back down. Not for anything.

Chapter 20

The walk back to Segerstrom Ranch is slow and uncomfortable. Tyse is a vague and hazy shape ahead of me, like a spirit leading me toward sanctuary. I listen as we walk, listen for the calls of mountain lions or the rumbling roar of a motorcycle, but there are only the sounds of the night, the rustle and quick chirps of night birds, the steady hum of crickets serenading the last of the warm air in the final nights before the first frosts come. When we reach the back door into the settlement, I'm almost surprised at how calm the night is, and I cross the distance to the shacks, barns and kitchen-house with a growing sense of confidence.

When I find Foxlight, he's still working with the Thuulhuum, hammering out the finer details of the part of the plan that involves securing the ranch, keeping it from falling apart while our little war party is away. I linger at his side as he talks, offer what I can, pick idly at a bowl of shelled walnuts and pine nuts that's being passed around. In the end, there's an uneasy sense of hope and resolve among the Thuulhuum, a faith in the chance we all have chosen to take. With lists in hand and every heart as settled as conversation and compromise can manage, we part and separate for the night, Foxlight and I retiring to our shack while the others disperse to their beds or leave to tackle their last minute duties.

I walk behind my chesnari as we go, watch the set of his shoulders, see the tension and the worry wire-taut and twisted up in his back. I say nothing, only put my hands on his shoulders, begin to knead as we reach the door.

"Wolf." He shakes his head, melts a little under my touch. Working quickly, I run my thumbs deep into his aching muscles, take advantage of the pause to loosen his lats and traps as much as I can. Breathing a deep sigh, he sinks into my hands, but I know it will end at any moment, that he'll pull away, take my wrists and hold me, focusing on what I might need instead of what he needs. It's a delicate balance – hitting hard and fast, overpowering him with deep tissue massage while I can, knowing he needs it, knowing it could end at any moment.

"Breathe, my love," I tell him, working my knuckles into a stubborn spot, rubbing at a tendon so tight I almost imagine I could play it like a guitar string. "Take a moment. Just breathe."

"Where did you go earlier?" he asks.

"To the woods," I whisper back. "West of here. I was seeking a vision."

"What did you see?"

I think about where to start, how to frame all of the images in my mind into words, into a cohesive narrative of the rise and fall of the machine mind, the birth of the Brass Dragon as Tyse sees it, the role of the raiders as tools or limbs of whatever has risen from the ashes of the fallen star. In the end, it all comes almost as word-vomit, bits and pieces falling together, but Foxlight only listens, takes in everything as I massage. At some point in the story, he leads me inside, listens as we strip away the layers of the day, climb into bed and curl up together. His eyes are calm but intent, watching me as I reveal everything, even the fears that Tyse has about the tattoos, about the captured hara of Segerstrom Ranch gaining tattoos of their own, being brainwashed or converted or turned into tools of the Brass Dragon somehow. Not once does he interrupt, and even as I start to run out of things to tell him, he nods, taking it all in.

"Do you think the hara in Imbrilim would change their minds if they knew?" I finally ask him.

"I doubt it." It comes simple, level. "Our tribe isn't afraid of machines. They have no reason to be. Most of the hara in Imbrilim and Immanion see machines of any kind only as simple tools, conveniences of a past age easily silenced with a sharp thought or a cunning wrench. If our superiors had an army of specialists and soldiers to spare, they'd probably send them, even if only to assess the situation more completely, but with our people spread so thin, this machine mind would seem more like a primitive, minimal threat, especially this far out in the middle of nowhere. Begging for support against something like the Brass Dragon, as you describe it, given the current state of the world, would be seen in the same light as asking for support in wrangling a wild tractor that ravaged a few crops and killed a farmer on the other side of the planet, or asking for help hunting down something fantastic of which there is little or no evidence, like an urban legend, or Bigfoot, while clear and present threats wait at the door."

"Humans discounted the existence of things that weren't widely seen or understood," I shoot back, trying to keep my tone even. "Hara have proved the stupidity of dismissing things that sound fantastic or incredible. We've manifested abilities that most human minds thought were fiction. How arrogant it would be to dismiss any enigma, no matter how unlikely, in the midst of a medium like a telepathic message!"

"I know," Foxlight says, puts a hand on my shoulder to

reassure me. "I agree."

"So what do we do?" I ask.

"Stick with the plan." Foxlight meets my eyes evenly. "Strike out against the orders of our superiors. Rescue Phelu and Cougar and all of the others. Assess the threat that the Brass Dragon may pose to the area and to the Gelaming, and then destroy it if necessary." He reaches up, strokes my cheek. There's a subtle tremor in his touch, just enough to show how much he's struggling against his own fears and doubts. "When the hara of Segerstrom Ranch have settled back into a comfortable routine, we'll personally bring our report on the situation to the Hegalion in Immanion and shock them with the stories of what we faced and what we overcame without any appreciable support from Imbrilim."

His brazenness is ridiculous, but it makes me chuckle. In the pause, I press my head against his chest, nuzzle there. In the moment, I feel my love for him keenly, feel his love radiating back in his warmth, his touch, his quiet laugh. In the moment, I want nothing more than to spend the rest of my life in his arms, bound up and safe, with not a thought given to the world beyond the walls.

"We should sleep, my love," he whispers into my hair, and I nod in reply, close my eyes. Holding me gently, oh so gently, he shifts toward the candle on the nightstand, snuffs it with a quick pinch of his fingers. The hot beeswax smell fills the little shack, and I pull it in, savor it, let it carry me on into the night, into dreams of spring flowers and the steady, surging heartbeat of the sea, of surf washing across the sand of a northwestern beach.

Chapter 21

The light of dawn comes too soon, and with it, the *sedim* from Imbrilim.

I hear the regal canter, the snorting of the horses long before they pass our shack. I hear the wonder of the hara of Segerstrom Ranch as they shout and gather – and then I hear other voices. Gelaming voices, cultured and quiet, and my heart jumps into my throat.

"Fox!" I shake my chesnari awake, kiss him as he rubs at his eyes, rises. "They're here!"

"The *sedim?*" he asks, blinking past the bleariness.

"Yes, and something more," I can't help but grin. Fox looks at me, sees the hope, the excitement in my eyes. "Gelaming," I add. "Warriors, maybe?"

"Warriors?" He squints, shakes his head.

"You said Imbrilim was sending just the *sedim*, right?" I look toward the door, want badly to bolt into the light and see how many *sedim* and Gelaming soldiers have arrived in Segerstrom Ranch. In my mind, I imagine a dozen, maybe more, armored and clad like knights, galloping out of the otherlanes and landing on the soft green grass outside, showing seriousness and splendor to impress the locals. "Two *sedim* for the recall, right? One for Hursi and Eagles, one for you and me?" I gesture toward the door. "I hear voices out there. Gelaming voices! Do you think somehar in Imbrilim finally listened and sent support?"

"It would be a true blessing if they have." Foxlight whips off the covers, quickly gathers his clothes and dresses. I follow his lead, do the same as quick as I can, have to leave my hair down and tangled to keep up with him. In a minute, we're outside the door, eyes casting about for the *sedim,* for the army we hope has arrived.

"Damn," Foxlight whispers. I follow his gaze, and my heart sinks a little at the sight. Up by the kitchen-house, two *sedim* stand quiet and regal, tails swishing. Their riders are dressed in formal, flowing white robes, with proud-crested ivory helms and long, curved ceremonial blades holstered at their sides. They aren't soldiers, look more like aides or functionaries, seem so out of place in the Gold Country, in the rural farmland squalor of Segerstrom Ranch. Beautiful but impractical, like a pair of sleek dehara cast in marble.

Hursi is the first to cross the distance, and as Foxlight and I hurry to meet with the newcomers, I see him reach up to one of the riders, take the har's hand in a gentle gesture, let it go again. There's conversation, but we miss most of it. By the time we reach the *sedim* and their riders, Hursi is already turning to face us, and his expression is far from encouraging.

"Hail!" Foxlight shouts. Both riders turn their *sedim* to face us, regard us evenly. "What news from Imbrilim? I was told we would be receiving a pair of *sedim* for our recall, but if I'd known that we would have guests as well, my chesnari and I would have prepared a meal to share with you."

"Your hospitality is kind, but we have already eaten," one of the Gelaming says. "I am Traekus, and this is Brykal." He gestures to the other rider.

"Foxlight and Tule Wolf." My chesnari gestures at himself and me. "What brings you to the distant hills of the Gold Country?"

"We are the vanguard for an evacuation force." Brykal looks at each of us in turn. "We were given orders to bring you and Twin Eagles back to Imbrilim first, then return with a force of twelve hara, who are being redirected from points in the far north and east of Megalithica for a quick extraction of everyhar else at this ranch."

"If Imbrilim can spare so many, even for one day..." I shake my head, hoping for something more. "Surely we can use a force of that size to track down and free Phelu."

"There's too much at stake." Traekus says it softly, reaches out and takes my hand in a compassionate gesture. "I can't imagine what it must be like for Twin Eagles, for one to lose somehar so close, but the orders from Arahal are clear and time is short. A complete and total extraction of everyhar from this ranch is the only option. There is room for both Gelaming and Thuulhuum in Imbrilim."

Foxlight looks at me, and in his eyes I see a swirling of fear and rage, just beneath the surface. The hara of our tribe have taken the decision out of our hands entirely, left us with only one choice. The choice to run, to abandon the Gold County and leave Phelu behind in the hands of the Brass Dragon. It's a choice he's refusing to accept.

"Gelaming *and* Thuulhuum?" Hursi folds his arms, squints at the two riders. "You realize that this ranch is home for the Thuulhuum, that they've spent years cultivating the land here, building infrastructure, building lives. Did it occur to anyhar in Imbrilim that the Thuulhuum might not *want* to leave with you?"

"It's not safe here." Brykal shakes his head, shows his palms as he tries to reason with Hursi. "Foxlight, even your own reports seem to state that anyhar who stays risks being abducted like all the others were."

"And what will you do if any of the Thuulhuum turn down your offer of a new life in Imbrilim? If they resist you?" Hursi is almost spitting fire now. "Will you abduct them like the raiders who struck here did? Will you drag them away in nets? Force them to surrender their heritage, their tribal identity and become Gelaming?"

"Control yourself! No har sane would stay here," Traekus announces, stern and solid. "The order to evacuate was given with an eye toward saving lives. If you would call yourself Gelaming, then act like it. Why do you fight this?"

"Because it's wrong." I shake my head. It feels ridiculously brash to say it, but I know Foxlight and Hursi feel the same way. All eyes are on me as I take a step forward, lock my own stare with Traekus's. "We decided as a group to stay here, to rescue those who were taken. When we leave, it won't be with you. It won't be on a *sedu* bound for Imbrilim. It'll be as a group, and we'll be following the trail left by the hara who violated this place."

"Operating in a dangerous area of Megalithica without support and against orders to evacuate would be foolish, beyond foolish!" Traekus's tone gets harsh, short. "Do you not understand? You've been *ordered* to return to Imbrilim for your own safety."

"If Imbrilim were really concerned about our safety, they would have sent soldiers to fight the raiders in these hills," Hursi growls. "They would have sent a force of fighting hara, and not just as a means to evacuate us conveniently, while the force is being redirected from the field and back to the city. Instead, they've sent you, a vanguard composed of a pair of self-important functionaries who would rather impress the backward locals with clean and shining ceremonial garb than wear something reasonable and functional."

The look Traekus shoots at him is ugly, a sneer that calls to memory all of the differences between the elite among the Gelaming and the misfits from the highways who some say only call ourselves Gelaming. Hursi doesn't let it get to him, not like I do, and when he speaks again, he smiles, offers his words almost as a challenge.

"Scowl all you like, Traekus. If you plan to take us, you'll have to take us gagged and trussed. We won't willingly abandon Phelu or the harlings of the Thuulhuum."

Brykal mutters something under his breath, and as the *sedim* start to shift and tap their hooves, the two riders glance at each other, exchange frustrated expressions.

"You won't change your mind?" Traekus asks.

"We won't," Foxlight says, his arms folded, stance solid and square.

"There will be consequences," Brykal adds.

"We know," I nod.

"Then, may the Aghama watch over you, guide you and keep you safe," Traekus offers, his temper cooling a little as he regards each of us in turn, then turns away sadly, urging his *sedu* into a trot toward the far eastern wall. As they leave, Brykal gives us all one last glance, shakes his head.

And then, as we watch, they rise into a gallop, flash through the walls of reality and back into the otherlanes, bound for Imbrilim with news I'm sure will come to haunt us when this is all over, when we return to the city to tell them of the Brass Dragon and all that we have yet still to see and live through.

If we return, I tell myself. In the pause, Foxlight puts one hand on my shoulder, squeezes like he knows, like he feels the same doubts, the same fear. *Maybe he does*, I decide, reach back and take his hand in mine.

Maybe he does.

Chapter 22

"Without the *sedim*, our plan starts to fall apart," Hursi says.

We're in the barn, the four of us, discussing options, while the Thuulhuum make final preparations. In less than an hour, the last of the loose ends on the ranch should be tied up. In less than an hour, the hara of Segerstrom Ranch will be armed and looking to us for a direction to march.

Foxlight crouches down next to Twin Eagles. "How's it look?"

Eagles sighs, wipes his hands on a torn rag. He's been picking at the motorcycle off and on since last night, tinkering with it. "Pretty standard hog." He knocks on the exhaust pipes with the head of a wrench. "Loud. Obnoxiously loud." He shakes his head. "Doesn't run on gas." He points at the tank. "I have no idea what it runs on. Looks like a bio-diesel of some kind, but as to what it's made from, your guess is as good as mine. I've never seen a set-up like this before. It's very clean. It looks new, but the engineering is very precise. These ferals must have a damn good mechanic, and access to a lot of high-performance old stock."

"Is there a way to make it quieter?" Foxlight asks. "Silent, maybe?"

"Well, if I had a welder, some steel pipe of the right size and some kind of insulation or steel wool..." Twin Eagles shrugs. "But it wouldn't be quiet enough. Gun the engine once and the whole county is going to know where you are. They were built to be loud. They were meant to attract attention, to be intimidating. The only way to keep one of these silent is to leave it turned off."

"Kind of nixes the idea of using it for scouting." Hursi looks across at me. "So, we just follow the trail as a group, walk right into whatever might be waiting for us?"

"No." Foxlight stands, shakes his head. "We'll need scouts, but they'll have to run on foot." He glances at me, then looks back to Hursi. "Of all the hara here, who moves the fastest through this kind of country? In your opinion."

"In my opinion?" Hursi folds his arms. "I'll volunteer to run ahead of everyhar. I can leave now, double back once I see what's ahead. I'll keep in touch, warn you with a brain-blip if I see anything on the road."

"I can go with him," Twin Eagles offers.

"You're too slow," Hursi shoots it down immediately.

Eagles grimaces, makes to say something, but Foxlight cuts him off."I need you with the bike," my chesnari says, nodding toward the hog. "We're bringing it with us. We'll keep it off and in neutral, walk it along as we go. It'll slow us down a little, but that might be good."

"Tyse is fast," I put in. Hursi looks at me, stares as if expecting more. "He knows the Gold Country well. He knows how to travel through the terrain here." I think about telling them about the run two nights ago, the rush that seemed so close to otherlane travel, but I'm not certain of it myself, can't expect them to believe it. *Hara moving through the otherlanes like sedim?* It seems impossible, even to me, even after what I've seen.

"I'll look for him," Hursi says, uncrossing his arms, adjusting his rifle strap. "I think I know what he looks like." He pauses, turns his eyes to Foxlight. "If I can't find him, I'm going alone. We'll need to hit the trail soon if we're going to get any kind of lead on the main group."

Foxlight nods. "Fair enough."

Hursi gives me and Twin Eagles one last glance, then turns and slips out. In the pause, my chesnari reaches out, settling a hand against my back. Smiling, I take his hand with mine, hold it palm to palm, fingers knitting together.

"I should get breakfast," Twin Eagles excuses himself, tries not to look at us. Suddenly self-conscious, Foxlight lets my hand go, puts a step between us. I wait until Eagles is gone, then close the distance again.

"Sorry," my Fox says. "I keep thinking about how much he must be hurting."

"I know." I take his hand, squeeze it gently. "We'll get Phelu back." I force every ounce of confidence I have into my words. "He's alive, and we'll get him back. I promise."

Foxlight looks at me then, his eyes searching mine. "Intuition? Something you've seen in a vision?"

"Yeah," I lie.

Foxlight turns away, sighs, but it's enough. It lifts a little of the weight from his shoulders, at least for the moment.

"We should get breakfast too," he says then, squeezing my hand back. "Could be a long road, long day."

Absently, I nod, follow him out of the barn and over to the kitchen-house. Already, my mind is elsewhere, tangled in the images of the visions that have come to me since I arrived in the Gold Country. When we pass a picnic table heaped with hunting rifles, I can't help but get a little nervous.

War is coming. War, and we're the ones who are bringing it to the Gold Country.

CHAPTER 23

When Hursi and Tyse come to say their goodbyes, I'm
chewing on a sandwich of fried eggs pressed between two
floppy pieces of acorn frybread and seasoned with spicy
ground bladderpod. Grease dribbles from the corner of
my mouth, and I wipe at it with a sleeve. Foxlight offers
Tyse a rifle and a handful of short, five-round clips, but he
turns it down. Before my chesnari can put it back with the
arsenal spread across the nearest picnic table, Hursi takes
the ammo, checks it, then shoves it into his rucksack.
"Never can have too many bullets," he says.

Tyse says nothing. He looks preoccupied, thoughtful.
When they leave, Hursi sets a swift pace, and the other
har matches it easily, keeps up with him even as they fling
themselves past the open doors of the palisade gate and
into the trees beyond.

Other hara approach the table, and Foxlight talks with
each of them in turn. Some are better with hunting rifles,
others have more experience popping cans and bottles
with handguns. My chesnari arms everyhar equally, does
all he can to pack their pockets and satchels with clips,
loose bullets, anything they think they can use. In each
case, he stresses conservation with every handful of
ammo he offers. "This is all we have," he says to each har.
"We don't know how many raiders are out there, how
long we'll be out there, if we'll have to hunt for food.
Every bullet counts. Remember that."

Everyhar understands. Even I get the lecture. The gun
he hands me is heavy, a twelve-gauge hunting shotgun
with the magazine plug taken out, so it holds ten rounds
instead of three. "Hard to miss with a shotgun," he says,

gives me a weak smile.

"Planning on putting me on the front line?" I ask, trying not to let my fear show.

"Hell no." He shakes his head, hands me a fistful of shotgun shells. "You and I will be with Eagles. Some hara lost their entire families in the raid. They've volunteered to be first contact, if there's a firefight." He pauses, swallows, looks away. "They've all got rifles with scopes. If we do this right, none of our hara will have to die."

"Rough being the leader of a war party, huh?" I try a little humor.

He gives me the edge of a laugh, grimaces, doesn't say anything more. I don't blame him. It's a grim duty, and there's so much that could go wrong. He's shouldering all of the blame already, letting it weigh him down.

"Hey," I say, try to massage the tension out of his shoulders, but he slips out of my hands, turns and pulls me into a hug instead.

"I'm sorry," he says, holding me close. I squeeze him back, hard as I can. We're both scared, uncertain and nervous. Neither one of us wants to be here, doing this, but there's a sense of duty that keeps us moving, a sense of what is right and what is wrong that keeps us focused on the rescue.

"Don't be sorry." I whisper the words in his ear, kiss his cheek as I hold him, start to sway gently. "This was my idea as much as it was yours. Hursi and Tyse and Eagles want this too. We all do." He nods against my shoulder, tries to hide the wetness already forming at the edges of his eyes. "Hey," I whisper. "Hey, hey. We can do this. Don't start digging any graves just yet. Like you said, if we do this right, none of our hara have to die."

"But they will." I can hear his strength cracking in the

whisper he breathes. "They will die. You and I both know that we're not all coming back from this alive."

I swallow, suddenly unable to string words together, to do more than sway and hold him. In my mind, I know he's right, but I'd never admit it out loud. At my shoulder, he sniffs, wipes his face against my shirt.

"You won't lose me." It takes a force of will for me to speak the words, to put them in air. When they come, they come quiet, almost meek. "I've got you, Fox."

"I've got you, Wolf," he echoes.

"We'll see this through to the end, together," I insist. "We'll have our house and our orchard and our couple of harlings yet. I promise."

"Something you've seen?" he asks me for the second time this morning, and for the second time, I lie to him.

"Yeah." The word tastes sour in my mouth, but I know he needs to hear it. "You'll see it too, soon enough. We'll see it together."

"Just got to get through this." He pulls in a deep breath, holds it.

"That's right." I pull away just enough to kiss him on the cheek, hold it and laugh when he tries for more. To him it looks playful as I dance out of his arms, grinning back at him, and that's fine. I know that he wants to share breath with me, but I also know that my heart is in turmoil. I don't trust myself enough to know I won't taint the sharing with fears, with the worries, the dark images that trouble my heart. "Think of tomorrow, or where we'll be in five years," I try, focusing on his eyes, his beautiful eyes, in an effort to keep my smile. "Keep that happy image in your heart, chesnari. Hold it, no matter what we face. Hold on to it, and know that we'll be living that life soon enough."

Chapter 24

We're a ragged-looking army, the ten of us.

In the center of the group, I help Eagles push the bike, keep it moving at a steady pace. Foxlight walks nearby, eyes on the trees, a high-power, Vietnam-era infantry rifle in his hands. It's an antique, sixty years old at least, and there were maybe twelve rounds for it in the whole settlement, but it's iconic, military black and intimidating. I've argued with him about it, about carrying something that fires twenty-two long rifle or four-ten birdshot instead, because we have boxes and boxes of those, but he carries it because he doesn't want to have to use it. That's what he says. He wants anyhar we encounter to take one look at him and his gun and decide that he's too deadly to tangle with. All I can think about is how nothing else in our little band fires 5.56 NATO. If he empties his magazine, his intimidating rifle won't be much more than a fancy shillelagh.

Derek, with his layers of decaying clothing, walks side-by-side at the front with Aldon, a har strapped up in pig-leather and bearskins, as massive as he is muscular. Both cradle scoped rifles, bolt-action thirty-aughts, with maybe thirty loose rounds between them and ten more strapped into each rifle's hand-tooled leather stock sleeve. The idea is that if we run into anything or anyhar on the road, they'll dive into the bushes and get crosshairs on it. With the two of them out of sight, four more of our group will step forward, make a line with the bike, Twin Eagles and I smack in the center. It's simple, and it leaves one har trailing behind to watch our back. Foxlight is the only one of our number not assigned a position. I guess everyhar figures that he's the de facto leader, that it's his job to do the talking and to go wherever he's needed. Still not sure how I feel about the risk involved with that.

The trail is weather-worn but substantial enough that it's easy to follow. Tread-ruts cutting deep into the mud of a deer trail lead us to a sparsely-graveled fire-access road where Derek and Aldon see enough mud and wear to keep us moving. Broken branches and long patches of flattened grass betray the trail when it thins, but things get challenging when the fire road dumps out onto the asphalt of a State Route. Mud flung from tracks marks a direction, and we follow it nervously, hoping Derek and Aldon are as competent at tracking as they seem to think they are.

Tracking bikes across asphalt turns out to be slow and tedious work. Derek and Aldon keep an eye out for intersections, for places where other fire-access roads merge into the State Route. Sometimes we have to stop while they argue and bicker over whether or not a pebble or a chunk of mud is new enough, or far enough from the asphalt to indicate our quarry left the road and went back into the woods. In the end, there's always some indication, some splintered twig or wear on the edge of a pothole that keeps us moving down the State Route, moving closer and closer to Cinder Hill.

At some point, Foxlight gets tired of standing around while Aldon and Derek spit and shout at each other. He calls a stop for lunch, and the spot he chooses is beneath a canopy of live oak that shades the packed dirt of an old driveway, which doglegs off the State Route. It's almost entertaining, breaking into the venison jerky and honeyed acorn bread, while our self-elected trackers argue over whether or not a rut on a gravel curb is small enough to have been left by a motorbike tire, but it also worries me a little. We've walked almost five miles in a stuttering, uncertain rhythm because of arguments like this, and they're getting more and more frequent the further we walk.

"This is a bad plan," Twin Eagles mutters, and I quickly shush him.

"It's our only plan," I shoot back, ignoring the unhappy look he gives me. I bite into a piece of bread to try to silence my own doubts, but they settle and nest in my mind anyway, chewing at me while I chew at my lunch.

"We'll hear from Hursi soon enough, I bet," Foxlight says. "Once he finds out where the raiders are hiding, he'll track back and guide us."

Twin Eagles grimaces. "Assuming he finds them – or manages to find us."

I try to make light of the situation. "I doubt he could miss us, with the way Aldon and Derek are arguing. I wouldn't be surprised if every har in the county knows where we are."

That gets a little smile from Eagles, or maybe just a grimace. It's hard to tell. On the asphalt, Aldon growls something sharp and cutting at Derek, stomps off down the road, pointing here and there, yelling indistinctly.

"Fucking clowns," somehar else mutters.

I tune it out, focus on my food. Eventually, Foxlight gets up, walks out to the road, peers down the eastern slope, up the western rise. Aldon and Derek are still arguing, but less so now that their focus is on my chesnari.

When Foxlight speaks, it comes sharp, firm,

commanding. "We're getting nowhere with all of this fighting. It's a safe bet that if they chose to take this road, they probably stuck to it for a while." He turns to our trackers. "Aldon! How long have you lived in this area?"

"All my life," he says. "I was born in the county, never left."

"What route is this?" Foxlight gestures at the road, looks it up and down, then fixes Aldon with a sharp, commanding stare. "Where does it run?

"J-95." Aldon gestures loosely east, then west. "Dead ends at Pine Lake Drive in Mi-Wuk, runs down past Jimtown on the other side, hooks out south toward the bayou and La Grange and everything out there."

"Hooks up with the Eighty-Eight just east of Cinder Hill," Derek puts in. "The closer we get to the city, the more roads the Ninety-Five crosses and runs with." He gestures, frustrated. "They've flung all their mud by this point. There's really nothing left to follow."

"I can track a garter snake through a pine grove," Aldon growls. "I'll get us to their front door, you can bet on that."

"You couldn't track a skunk in the open if it sprayed itself," Derek spits back. "I still say they left the Ninety-Five two miles back and went out Bald Mountain Road. There's hillbilly gun ranges and houses and hell, the whole town of Dambacher is out there."

"You're a damn fool, Derek." Aldon makes a sharp, angry gesture. "Ain't nothing out there but trees and busted buildings. I saw at least a dozen of those hogs the other night. Looked like a goddamned motorcycle gang. You really think they're gonna stash their rides in a gutted pit like Dambacher?" He stomps, fumes. "Did you *not* see the mark on that damn curb? That's fresh rubber, Derek!

Fresh burned rubber!"

"Fresh burned rubber, my ass," Derek snarls. "I've got your fresh burned rubber swinging–"

"Alright!" Foxlight roars. Both of the trackers fall silent, turn in surprise. His eyes flick from one to the other, teeth bared. "You're acting like a couple of rotten human children. Dammit! You can do better than this! We all need you to do better than this!"

"I told you," Derek throws back. "We can't track them on this–"

"I don't want to hear it," my chesnari snarls, glaring. When he turns to Aldon, the bear-har straightens up instantly, eyes wide. "Aldon! From now on, you do the tracking. *All* of the tracking." He turns back to Derek. "You! I want you walking rear with Wright."

"Yeah, but–"

"Shut up!" Foxlight commands, stabbing a finger toward the east. "I don't want to hear another word out of you–"

"Fuck you, Gelaming!" Derek growls suddenly, cutting him off. "Aldon is gonna get us all lost and you're gonna get us all killed." He stands there fuming for a moment, then spits and stomps. "You know what? No, fuck this. I didn't lose nobody when the ferals hit us. I got no reason to be here. I'm headed back to the ranch. Y'all crazy fuckers can follow the Gelaming to your deaths if you want. I'm going home."

My jaw drops in shock. For a moment, we all just sit there staring, watching as Derek shoulders his rifle and marches off back toward Segerstrom Ranch. In the pause, somehar stirs, and then I see two other hara shoulder their guns, start off after Derek.

Reflexively, I look at Foxlight, catch the panic in his

eyes. He's losing control of the situation fast, and he's painfully aware of it.

"Derek!" I try, but he doesn't turn, doesn't answer. It takes me a moment to remember the names of the other two hara following him, but when I do, I call out to each of them in turn. "Dayvin!" I shout. "Sarlfurd!"

Neither turns, neither stops. I shake my head as my voice stalls in my throat. When I finally force myself to call out again, it comes hoarse, and I hate how desperate it sounds. "Wait!"

But they don't wait, and they don't look back. Fists shaking, I stand and stare side-by-side with my chesnari, but there's nothing either of us can do. In another ten minutes, the three Thuulhuum are gone, rounding the curve of a switchback and passing out of sight beyond a row of trees. Lost, frustrated, Foxlight hangs his head, sighs, rubs at his eyes.

We're three less now, I keep thinking. *An army of seven, untrained and under-equipped.*

And in the silence, I close my eyes, wonder, for what feels like the millionth time, if we're all very brave for doing this, or just very stupid.

CHAPTER 25

I hate that we make better time with Derek gone, but we do. For better or worse, putting all of our faith in Aldon's tracking skills keeps us moving, puts us almost to the city limits of Cinder Hill before the wet winds and heavy clouds moving in from the west start to gather into an ominous storm. "Rain tonight," somehar says, and for the first time in a while, the thought of rain makes me grimace.

"We should find shelter," Foxlight says, addressing Aldon more than anyhar else. The bear-har turns back, nods, but doesn't say a word.

When the Ninety-Five dumps into the Eighty-Eight, Aldon leads us a little way along the larger highway, then backtracks, turns us off a side road. "There's more recent rubber down there." He points toward surface streets that cut straight lines between parking lots and hollowed-out structures collapsing under their own weight. A deep groove in the asphalt gives him reason to choose another side-road, and soon we're picking our way southwest, around the perimeter of Cinder Hill.

By the time dusk sets in, it's already drizzling. We watch the rain from the broken husk of a brick building, bust out a chunk of the tile floor and build a fire with the rotten wood underneath. It isn't much of a fire, mostly smoke that billows black against the roof above us, but it gives us a little more than body heat to work with. When the rain starts coming down in thundering sheets, flooding the streets outside, we huddle together, cluster into one big shivering, nervous knot.

Sleep doesn't come easily, doesn't linger. For what seems like hours, I sit propped up between Fox and Eagles, staring out into the night, wondering when the rain will stop, if it *will* stop. In my best moments, I feel as foolish as a child playing soldier in a genuine warzone. In my worst, I contemplate packing up and heading back to Segerstrom Ranch, dragging Foxlight with me. The most I do is sigh and tuck my face into the space between my chesnari's neck and shoulder.

Dawn comes, and with it, the grumbling. The rain is still pounding the streets, running like rivers across slick asphalt, and nohar has any interest in going out in it. One by one, hara start to wake and bicker, and it just makes me want to hide in Foxlight's warmth all the more. Already, the Thuulhuum are starting to question Aldon's ability to track anything after a night of heavy rain, and I can't blame them for their doubts. I've been wondering for a while how much oil, grime and rubber there can really be on the road, how much of it might really be new, or even from our ferals. Aldon has no reason to lie to us, no reason I can think of, but still the doubts chew at me, and I find myself thinking of Derek, of Dayvin and Sarlfurd, thinking of Derek's words, his resolve.

"You're not really leading us to the ferals, are you, Aldon?" Somehar asks suddenly. I try to ignore the voice, but Foxlight looks up, turns, listens.

Aldon is silent for a long moment, and then I hear a sigh, the scuffle of somehar getting to their feet.

"We're not going to find them," he says, and I can hear the hesitation in his voice. "They're gone, and the only way we'd see them again is if we were up at the ranch when they come back, looking to pick up the few of us they missed."

"So what – you led us out here? For what?" Another har asks.

Aldon is quiet for a moment, seems to consider his words, then says: "There were signs at first, but then–" He hesitates, pushes through. "Derek was right. I thought maybe if we just kept walking, we'd see something, hear something, or Hursi would show up and point us in the right direction, but it never worked that way. We just kept walking, and then the rain..." He lets the sentence trail off, leaves it hanging in the silence.

For a long moment, nohar speaks. Only the rain is there to rail against the silence. I look up, see Aldon half-turned away, head hung low, nervously wringing water out of his bearhide rags.

"Bullshit!" Somehar shouts. It's explosive, full of fire and rage. I lean into Foxlight, turn to see, spot one of the Thuulhuum standing, fists clenched.

"Helzer," Foxlight calls the har by name, tries to calm him.

The look Helzer shoots him is vicious, momentary. When he turns on Aldon again, the har is bearing teeth, practically spitting. "I oughta shoot you where you stand, Aldon! Shoulda listened to Derek!" He's addressing everyhar now. "We all should have listened to Derek!"

"We're here, now." Foxlight takes a moment to carefully untangle himself from me, rises to stand equal with Helzer. Sitting at my chesnari's feet, I look up at him, watch as his eyes meet mine, then move to Wright's and Jaylin's before rising again to fix with Helzer's. "It took us a day to reach Cinder Hill. Aldon did what he believed was best, and we followed him in good faith. It's raining now, and everyhar is in a bad mood. Let's take a moment to think about what we can do."

"That's what you'd like, isn't it?" Jaylin spits. "This was your plan, Gelaming. Follow Aldon, find the ferals." He shakes his head. "Worked out real well so far, huh?" He turns to Helzer and Wright. "I don't even know why we're following this asshole."

"It wasn't just *his* plan." I stand, can't remain silent any longer. "Everyhar here wanted this. Everyhar here has somehar they lost in the raid, and everyhar here is angry and hurting and out for blood. What would you have done if we hadn't been here? If you'd have been on your own when the raiders came? Would you have stayed at Segerstrom Ranch, waiting for the next raid, or would you be out here, in the rain and the ruins, pissing and moaning and blaming somehar else for it?"

Jaylin looks away, hugs his knees to his chest and starts to rock. My eyes lock with Helzer's, and for a moment he keeps his rage, but when it starts to fizzle, he stomps away, finds a wall to plant his hand against, leans, cursing.

"Wright," Foxlight regards the one Thuulhuum har who has stayed silent the whole time. "What do you think we should do?"

The question catches the young har off guard, and it takes him a moment to collect his thoughts. "Well," he tries, standing quickly, stumbling a little. "If we can't find them, then maybe we can get them to find us." He licks his lips, hesitating, then looks over to Aldon. "Aldon, how far into Cinder Hill do the signs go? When was the last time you were sure about the trail?"

"When the Ninety-Five merged into the Eighty-Eight," he says, still wringing his bearskins. "Maybe a quarter mile east of there."

"So, not that long ago." Wright nods, looks at the

motorcycle, then at Foxlight. "What if we made a lot of noise? Maybe if we really rev that thing up, they'll hear it and come looking. We can set a trap, or maybe just hide and leave the bike for them to find, then follow them back to wherever they've come from."

"I like the second idea," Foxlight says, then turns to Twin Eagles. "Can you make the bike louder?"

"Louder's easier than quieter." Eagles smiles a little. "Anybody got a hacksaw?"

"I doubt it," Aldon blinks, then looks at the bike. "I can think of another way to punch a hole in those pipes, though." He gestures at his thirty-aught, propped against a nearby wall. "High-powered rifle'll do it. That or a brick. Hit it enough times with a brick and I bet you'll knock something loose."

"It's either that or a cutting torch." Eagles looks out beyond the walls and into the rain. "If we get some distance on the bike and let Aldon put a couple of holes in the pipes, we might get the extra volume you're looking for."

"Plus the noise of the gun." Foxlight gestures. "Seems like a pretty sure shot with a scope. Doesn't matter if he misses and hits a tire or something. As long as the bike runs and roars, that's all that matters."

"So, all we need now is a good place to hide, and a good place out in the open where we can put the bike," Wright puts in.

"And a way to rev it at a distance," I add.

"Machines are easy. Just a matter of tugging the right cable." Twin Eagles grins, taps his forehead with two fingers. "Once it's running, I can open the throttle up with my mind and make her roar so loud they'll hear her in the next county over."

"Let's get everything set-up," Foxlight says, taking on the firm, assured tones of the leader we all want him to be. "Jaylin, Helzer, you're with me and Tule Wolf. Let's find a place to hide while Aldon, Wright and Eagles figure out the bike."

CHAPTER 26

The rain is still pouring down when Wright, Aldon and Eagles walk the bike to the soaring overpass of the Eighty-Eight that curves along the eastern perimeter of Cinder Hill. It's a high spot, out in the open, and Eagles reasons that the sound of the pipes will resonate through the concrete of the overpass and carry all the further, even through the muffling effect of the rain. On the ground, Foxlight and I search out every concrete culvert in the area that hasn't been smashed or blocked, choose two that are hidden behind enough scraggly brush and debris to make them decent for hiding. When Aldon's gun goes off, everyhar stops, looks, waits. Four shots ring out through the rain, two in the neck of each pipe. Each puncture is clean, precise. The loudness of the gun makes me nervous, makes me move faster, but not as fast as I move when Eagles kicks the bike to life, gives it that first little bit of throttle just to hear it spit and grumble.

We're all soaked through completely by the time we gather in one of the culverts. It's the larger of the two, almost big enough for all of us to stand upright inside, and the only one with a clear view of the overpass and the motorcycle. Shoes slosh and squeak as we try to stick to the mossy walls, try to keep out of the rainwater rushing through the center of our hiding place. Shivering as much as the rest of us, Foxlight gives Twin Eagles the nod to open the throttle on the bike, and with the storm picking up, blowing a cold, howling wind through the ruins around us, I wonder if the roar will be loud enough, if we'll even hear it down here.

When Twin Eagles closes his eyes and reaches out through the storm with his mind, the rest of us wait with bated breath. Silence stretches, and then I wonder if he's over-estimated his abilities, if tugging that one tiny cable from several hundred yards away is more than he can manage. Hesitant to say anything, I bite my lip, glance at Foxlight, but my chesnari doesn't look back. Eyes closed, he stands there silently waiting, maybe praying.

And then the roar of the hog splits the storm wide open, like the angry howl of some massive, elemental beast. It's startlingly loud, rolls over and through everything in vibrating waves. Grinning, Twin Eagles pulls the cable with his mind again and again, opens up the throttle until the bike is screaming on the overpass, announcing itself with a voice all fire and fury. Nature seems to take note, echoes back with the rumble of thunder, but the bike is still louder. A pace or two away from Eagles, Wright and Helzer chuckle and howl in unison with the engine. "If they don't hear *that*," Aldon says, "I'll eat my bearskins right here in this culvert."

Minutes pass, build into hours. The rain falls harder and harder, falls so hard that it cuts visibility to almost nothing. Eagles lets the bike putter and idle here and there, guns it in spurts, but no other engine noise echoes back in answer when he does. The excitement of the moment, of that first fiery roar passes quickly, and as the sky gets darker, and the water in the culvert rises higher, our meager group of would-be soldiers huddles together for warmth, says little, and none of it is positive. After a while, even the roars of the motorcycle seem half-hearted, Eagles opening the throttle less and less with each pull.

And then it happens. Silence. Eagles drifts, looks confused for a moment, and then his eyes go wide.

"Shhh," he says quickly, cutting us off before anyone can speak. "It's not running anymore."

"Did it run out of fuel?" Foxlight whispers back.

"I don't know." Eagles rises slowly, shakily, pressing his back against the wall of the culvert for support. "Didn't sound or feel like it was running rough, running low." He swallows, tries to press down the fear I can see rising up in him. "It feels like – it feels like somehar *turned it off.*"

Aldon is closest to the mouth of the culvert. Foxlight looks at him, gestures, and the bear-har nods back in response, his hands white-knuckling his rifle. In the silence that follows, we all watch Aldon creep to the edge of the opening, crouch and peer out toward the overpass.

I bite my lip again. Aldon shifts in his crouch, raises his rifle, brings the scope to his eye. The silence stretches, then turns almost ominous. When Aldon lowers his rifle again, he turns, looks at me, gestures.

I don't wait. I splash through the water in the culvert, cross to stand beside him, take the rifle as he hands it to me. I'm half out in the rain, have to wipe the water from the lens to see through the scope. Concrete fills my vision as I search, raise the crosshairs to the overpass, to the bike–

And then I see it. A figure, hazy and vague in the mist and heavy rain. I blink, rub at my eye, wipe the scope down with a sleeve and look again. Clothes come into focus, a gun, slung off one shoulder, and then the har turns, looks toward us, toward me.

"Hursi!" Foxlight whispers even before I can. I feel it, and as I look past the rifle and back into the culvert, I can see that Twin Eagles feels it too. The mind-touch, the mental *hello, I'm here* that we've all come to recognize.

"It's him on the overpass." I hand the rifle back to Aldon. "Maybe he's figured out where the raiders are."

Foxlight and Eagles are already grinning as we climb out of the culvert and up the side of the brush-choked gully that runs into it. I can't blame them – it's the first bit of hope we've had in hours, a day, and it's got me grinning too. We move silently, don't shout or call out, but he feels the mental touches we send back to answer his, stands watching us, waving from the other side of the concrete barricade. When we're all out in the open, he backtracks to the exit, hurries down and meets us on the surface streets. Before we even reach him, I can see that he's limping a little, favoring one leg, his right arm bandaged up tight with duct tape and strips of old torn rags.

"What happened?" Foxlight asks as we all come together in the center of an intersection, blinking and shivering against the rain.

Hursi says nothing, simply gestures at the husk of a building, takes off toward it. We follow him without question, but the injuries worry me. Uncertain, I look to Foxlight as we run, and he takes my hand to reassure me, squeezes it. He's still grinning, and it brings a little of my smile back with it.

Once we're under the cover of a roof and out of the rain, Foxlight asks the question that's been brewing in my mind since I spotted Hursi through the scope of Aldon's rifle. "Where's Tyse?"

"Segerstrom Ranch," Hursi says, wiping the rain out of his eyes with his one mobile arm. "Or halfway there, probably. He's gone back to get the feral." Hursi pauses to catch his breath, swallows. "A lot's happened. I've got a great deal to tell you."

I reach out, touch the bandage. "Let's start with the arm."

"Oh, this?" Hursi grins. "We found the gang that hit the ranch. One of their hara was walking perimeter. He and I had a bit of a tussle."

"Looks like you won." Aldon grins behind us. "Hate to see what the other guy looks like."

"He's got a few bruises, but he'll live," Hursi says, moving his tightly-wrapped arm a little. "He helped with the bandages, actually." Hursi looks to Foxlight again. "They aren't what we thought. I've been inside their camp. I've talked to them." His eyes flick to mine, to Twin Eagles', to Helzer's and Wright's. "They want to ally with us. They want to forge an alliance with the Gelaming *and* the Thuulhuum."

CHAPTER 27

For a long moment, nohar says anything. We're all too shocked, all too stunned.

"An Alliance!?" Jaylin finally breaks the silence, spits. "They raid us, set fire to our buildings, carry off two thirds of our people, and now they want a fucking *alliance?*" He sneers, shakes his head. "I hope you told them to fuck off."

"Like I said, they aren't what we thought," Hursi says, his eyes sticking with Foxlight. "Our hara have been treated well. They're healthy, they're happy. This whole thing was just one big misunderstanding." He makes a dismissive gesture. "I know it sounds unbelievable. Tyse was there with me. He can confirm it when we meet with him."

"So when do I get my chesnari back?" Twin Eagles pushes through Foxlight and I to stand before Hursi. "If they're so friendly, then why isn't Phelu with you? Why isn't he here!?"

"Because it's dangerous out here," Hursi says, his tone suddenly serious, almost dire. "There is a threat here in the Gold Country, but it isn't the feral hara who hit Segerstrom Ranch. It's something far worse that we need to be worried about. It's something bigger, something alien, and it has a taste for the flesh of our kind. It's eaten their hara, and they're afraid that if the group of our hara they're protecting try to journey back to Segerstrom Ranch, they'll be attacked and eaten too."

"We haven't seen anything strange on the road," I put in, attracting nods and glances from the others. "Nothing has tried to attack us."

"Not yet." Hursi fixes me with a sharp stare. "There's a reason I turned off the bike. Noises like that attract it. It mostly hunts around Cinder Hill, and mostly at night." He gestures to the crumbling walls of the building. "We're exposed here, and if it decides to attack tonight, we'll all likely be killed. Segerstrom Ranch might be safe, maybe, but it's too far away for us to get there in time."

"And so our only option is to seek sanctuary with the gang hara before nightfall?" I ask. I hate the idea, and maybe that's what's making me uneasy, making me feel like this whole thing is wrong or off somehow. On impulse, I reach out, touch his cheek, feel it with my fingers, but there's nothing unusual there, no tattoo, no brass filaments, nothing beneath the surface. He's lucid, convincing, easy to trust.

And that bugs me. Really bugs me.

"I'm not one of them." Hursi watches me with those intent, piercing eyes. "You're looking for the gang markings they wear, right? The weird tattoos?"

"Yeah." I let my arm drop back to my side. I blink, hesitate for a moment, considering. Beside me, my chesnari watches me as if studying my expression, trying to read me.

"If this thing is so deadly, then how have you survived?" Helzer finally asks.

"Luck," Hursi says, meeting the other har's eyes. "Being cautious, being quiet, and being very lucky."

Helzer scoffs at the response, stalks away. I glance at Aldon, catch his attempts to cover his nervousness and fear with a smile. Twin Eagles still stands with his arms folded, his eyes dark, untrusting.

Wright breathes a frustrated sigh. "Well, we wanted

the Ferals to find us." Looking at me, then at Foxlight, he shakes his head, spreads his hands in an open gesture. "They've found us. I say we go with Hursi."

"And if it's a trap?" Jaylin asks.

"We can divide into two groups," Foxlight offers, "One group will wait–"

"No," Hursi cuts him off. "Anyhar who stays behind will die. You haven't seen this thing in action. I have." He swallows, looks at each of us in turn. "The amount of noise you've made today, I'm surprised it hasn't killed all of you already."

"So if we go, we all go?" Foxlight asks.

"Like I said," Hursi looks at him, holds the stare. "You haven't seen how this thing hunts. It's vicious, sadistic. Anyhar who stays behind *will* be torn apart and *devoured*."

Aldon straps his rifle in against his shoulder. "Let's go, before it gets any later."

"I'm with Aldon," Twin Eagles uncrosses his arms, nods. His eyes are still dark and angry, but something has changed in them. On some level, I understand, swallow, then wrap my arms across his shoulders and nod to Hursi.

"If we go, we all go." I try to keep my iron. *It's Hursi,* I remind myself. *Our guardian angel.* His story is wild, improbable, but I can't seem to poke any holes in it. He has an answer for everything. Foxlight looks at me and I look back, meet his eyes evenly for a moment before turning to Hursi again. "We'll go. Lead the way."

CHAPTER 28

Even limping and bandaged, Hursi moves fast. It isn't easy keeping up with him, following him through the rain into the crumbling streets of Cinder Hill. As we run, I notice things. Little things. Strange things. The long grooves at railroad crossings, where the steel rails have been excised without a trace left behind. The total lack of screws, nails, plastic trash, anything synthetic. Wood, brick, bone – there's no shortage of that, but Cinder Hill looks like somehar has sucked all of the rubber, all of the metal and plastic out of it and left it to crumble under its own weight. It's strange, unnerving, and then we round the last bend before downtown and I realize something–

The machines, the drones of the machine-mind. They're *gone*. Every last one of them.

"Hursi!" I struggle to close the distance between myself and him. He doesn't slow, even as I whisper: "This thing hunting hara in these hills. Is it a machine?"

"It's something more." Hursi doesn't look at me, doesn't offer any additional insight.

"It's taken the drones, hasn't it?" I push. "The machines that were here, dead in the streets. It's done something with them."

Hursi looks at me then, but says nothing. When he stares ahead again, he seems worried, uncertain. I swallow against my own nervousness, follow his lead.

Once we're in the sagging ruins of downtown Cinder Hill, Hursi hooks into a side street. All around us, there are gaps in the dead grass, so many gaps, as if all the machines that had been lying dead or dormant for the past six years suddenly stood up and marched away in the middle of the rain storm. It's all I can do to keep moving, and with each step I feel the heavy, pressing weight of fear and worry seeping into the dampened spirits of every member of our ragged little band.

Every one of us except Hursi.

I put the thought out of my mind, refuse to follow it. After a few more hundred yards, he leads us across and down a few more side streets until we reach one that dips toward a gully. As we get closer, he whistles, and then a hulking, muscular har strapped into biking leathers studded with spikes, patches and pins climbs up onto the road from the gully, looks at us, gestures for us to follow. I glance back at Foxlight, but his expression is utterly unreadable. For now, all I can do is stick close to Hursi and keep a firm grip on my shotgun.

Deer trails and tread-ruts cut meandering lines down through the dead grass and into the gully. Below us and near the bottom, a little concrete ledge sits about two feet off the rocky, burbling breakers of a shallow creek. Near it, set into the side of the gully, I spot an archway of concrete and chunks of rough, natural stone that wrap around a door of iron bars secured with thick chains and a padlock. The har in studded biking leathers pulls a rusty key from a breast pocket and unlocks the door, doesn't try to muffle the clang and rasp of the chain or the rusty hinges that secure the bars to the inside of the archway. Hursi nods at me, then turns and passes through the door, out of sight. The har at the entrance lets him pass with his rifle slung, but stops me as I reach the threshold, blocks my path with one meaty arm.

"Gun," he says. It's simple, direct, sounds raw, rough, like he's only recently learned how to speak. He holds out his other hand, stares at me in silent expectation.

Nervous, I glance back at Foxlight, get a wary look in return. Options flit through my mind, quick and daring, but then I hear Hursi's voice in the dimness beyond the door.

"You'll get it back," he reassures me. "You're being invited into their home, and all they ask is that you leave your weapons with them while you stay."

I swallow. I want to argue with him. I want to sit in the wet grass of the gully with my arms crossed and protest with silence and glares until they let us take our guns inside, but I know it isn't going to happen.

Foxlight breathes a tired sigh, unslings his infantry rifle and pushes it into the muscular har's hands. I watch him helplessly as he passes me, follows Hursi into the earth. Aldon goes next, gives up his rifle, and Wright follows him.

The muscular har watches me sharply, warily, and as more of our rifles and pistols are pushed onto him, I can't help but feel the pressure of being the only har to hold out. I feel like a livestock animal hesitating at the door of the slaughterhouse, while all of the others are led inside. Only Twin Eagles stops to wait with me, stands side-by-side with me, looking the big biker up and down as if sizing him up.

"What do you think, Wolf?" He asks, turns to meet my eyes directly. I look away at first, but eventually I steel myself, take a deep, steadying breath and raise my gaze to his.

"I think Phelu's in there." I push my shotgun at the muscular har with enough force that I feel the steel slap against his meaty hands. I don't look at him, don't care about his reaction. My eyes stay with Twin Eagles's. "I know Foxlight is in there. Whatever happens, at least we'll all be together when it does."

"Good enough for me," Eagles says, and I can tell he's trying to quash the shakiness in his own voice. Drawing out the revolver he's been carrying since we left Segerstrom Ranch, he hands it to the muscular har, takes my hand as soon as he's relieved of the gun. Together, we turn, walk through the archway and into the dimness.

And I try not to flinch when I hear the bars slam closed behind us, the chain drawing across iron like the pull of a saw, the finality in the heavy click of the lock as it closes.

Chapter 29

Eagles and I stick close as we make our way down the narrow passage. Absently, I reach out, run my hand along the river-worn stones embedded in the concrete walls, the arch that curves just a few inches overhead. Light is scant, comes from old-style oil lamps set in sconces at intervals along the wall. I can't help wrinkling my nose as we go deeper. I don't know what the lamps are burning, but their oily smoke smells putrid, fecal. At times, it almost makes me gag, but we press on past each lamp, follow footsteps until the passageway opens into a wide room packed with workbenches and the kind of loud, thundering motorcycles that roared out of the night when Segerstrom Ranch was hit. Another har looks at us, directs us toward a side-passage with a firm but silent gesture, and in the half-light, I see the glitter of his facial tattoo, so similar to the others, brassy and eye-catching.

The side passage isn't much bigger than the entrance, and soon drops down into a long flight of shallow, stony stairs. It's claustrophobic how low Eagles and I have to duck to continue down the staircase, but I swallow past the spinning, the budding nausea. We're close to Phelu and the others. We must be. Up ahead, I can hear talking, the echoes of indistinct pieces of conversation bouncing back through the thick, damp air.

We must be a hundred feet beneath Cinder Hill when the staircase ends abruptly, opens to a wide natural cavern reinforced with almost two-hundred years of care. Dark logs that look like the trunks of oak trees sealed in wax or tar hold most of the weight of the earth above them, but iron beams with rust-weeping rivets and concrete retaining walls reinforce the frontier architecture of the Old West. Looking around, I see that it's like an intersection in a mine, that it moves in five different directions, and two of those directions are sealed over with rubble, collapsed and dusty.

"Here," Hursi calls, attracting our attention to one of the side passages. Foxlight and the others stand with him in the mouth of the tunnel, and it's wide enough for them to spread out into a loose group. Hell, three cars could park side-by-side in the tunnel with room to spare. It's that big.

Trying not to be drawn in too much by the size of the cavern and the tunnels, Eagles and I join the others, follow Hursi as he leads us deeper. The floor is rough-cut stone, with wear patterns from feet and pack animals. I can't help but wonder what it might have been like down here a hundred years ago, what the purpose of these tunnels might have originally been. It doesn't look like a mine, but maybe–

There's a sound, a scuff in the shadows, and instantly, it puts me on guard. My eyes dart into the darkness, look for movement, and then somehar melts out of the wall and walks right up to Eagles and I.

It's all I can do not to call out, to say something, but the shape – the har – holds a finger to his lips and gestures quickly before disappearing into darkness again. Stopping, glancing at Hursi, I realize he's preoccupied, that the group is getting further and further from us as we linger. When I look into the shadows again, I make out the curve of another adjoining tunnel, a smaller passage cut roughly into the rock, barely big enough to stand up in. Reflexively, I grab Eagles by the wrist, gesture for silence, lead him into the darkness. In any other circumstance, it might feel foolish, even stupid, but I recognize the har who approached us, who melted back into that earthen night just as quickly as he came.

"Tyse," I whisper, flinch as he appears again, wide-eyed and with his finger still pressed against his lips, urging silence. Eagles cups a hand over his own lips in surprise, and as Tyse gestures for us to follow him, I look back toward the light, just quickly, to make sure nohar's noticed us.

Tyse moves quickly through the twisting, tight-walled cavern. We almost have to run to keep up with him. It isn't easy muffling our steps, but we try, try to be as silent as the har we're chasing. Only the swish of his heavy cloak comes back to us, dusting the floor, brushing against the walls. When the passage bends suddenly, Tyse stops, throws back the hood of the cloak and reaches out, grabs us both by our shirts. He's scared, worried. His eyes dart over us, search our skin, our cheeks.

"How long have you been here?" he asks.

Eagles shakes his head, opens his mouth.

I beat him to the answer. "A few minutes." I shake my head. "Tyse! What are you doing here? Hursi said you'd gone back to Segerstrom Ranch."

"Hursi is one of them." The words spill from Tyse's mouth. He's panicked, not thinking clearly.

I reach out, wrap a hand in his cloak. "What are you saying?" My eyes search his face. "He doesn't have a tattoo. How can he be one of them?"

"The Brass Dragon." Tyse's gaze locks with mine. "It's learning, evolving still. The tattoos, the ferals – those are prototype drones. They're early, brutish attempts. Simple puppets, almost human. Hursi is something more. What it has done to Hursi runs so much deeper, is so much more complex."

"What is he saying?" Eagles demands, wide-eyed. "What is he saying? Where is Phelu!?"

"There isn't much time." Tyse shakes his head. "Hursi will notice that you're missing and come looking for you. He can't know I'm here."

"I need more than that," I shoot back, my eyes chasing his as he tries to look away. "I need a plan, Tyse. You know these hara better than we do. What's your plan?"

"Plan?" he scoffs, swallows. "I only have one idea, and it's stupid."

"Tell us!" Eagles demands.

"Kill it. Kill the Brass Dragon," Tyse snaps. His eyes flick to Twin Eagles', dart back to mine.

"How?" I ask.

Tyse swallows again. "There's a way that Stoff and I killed the machines. There's a thing I can do if I can get close enough to it, to the brain of the thing that's running all of this. It's like magic, but it works." He pauses, breathing fast. "I need a distraction. I need somehar to keep Hursi and the ferals back while I reach out and interface with the machine mind."

"Interface?" Twin Eagles shakes his head. "How?"

"It's hard to explain." Tyse fights with words in the pause, makes a gesture like he's trying to capture something, finally bites his lip and blasts an exhale through his nose. "It just works. I've done it before, and it's the only thing that I know that works."

"Wolf? Eagles?" The sound of my chesnari's voice echoes back through the darkness, through the cavern, and for the first time in my life, it sends a shiver down my spine, chills my blood. Tyse shushes us, then turns and scurries away, darting for the shadows. Reflexively, I turn, grab Eagles by the collar and drag him back toward the larger cavern.

Hursi is the first thing we see when we stumble back into the light, and I swear that when I meet his eyes, he knows. *He knows.* His stare is level, direct, pierces me like the point of a knife. I can't help but look away, end up glancing to the side. My chesnari steps up suddenly, and the sight of him swells my heart immensely.

"Fox!" His name explodes from me. I don't think, just rush him, pull him close, half-dragging Eagles with me. Somewhere in the middle of the hug, I feel ridiculous, fall away a little, struggle to find words. "I – we saw a – we saw something, a thing, a shiny *thing*, and we got lost..." I let the words trail off. I can't help glancing at Hursi to see if he'll buy the lie, end up staring, looking for signs that he's being controlled somehow, that he's something other than the hunter, the Gelaming and friend I thought I knew.

"Stay close," Hursi says, meeting my eyes evenly. "These tunnels run deep under the Gold Country. Some of them run for miles. It'd be easy for a har to get lost down here and never be seen again."

I swallow, try not to see the threat in his words, but I swear that it's there. He watches me for a moment more, hawklike, then turns, starts walking again. "Come on." He gestures. "The others are just up this way."

"Phelu," Twin Eagles whispers, clutches my hand as hard as I'm clutching Fox's. When we move, we move in a knot, and I know that Foxlight is uneasy, that he's picking up on my erratic fear, my wide-eyed panic. I want to tell him everything, want to tell him about Tyse, but I keep it packed down. Whatever is going to happen will happen soon. Just have to ride it out. Just have to ride it out and trust.

And as we walk deeper into the underground complex, I look back at intervals, swear I see a shape moving through the shadows, darting, crouching, following as silently and discreetly as he can.

Chapter 30

"It's just up this way," Hursi says. The tunnel we've been following runs straight ahead as far as we can see, but after maybe a few hundred yards, he leads us off into another passage that slopes upward and closes in, until it's only about ten feet from wall to wall. Next to him, Aldon glances back at the distance we've covered, and I can see in his eyes that he's worried.

"Sure is a long way." Helzer glances back at me, lets his eyes rise and crawl across the walls.

"Most of the hara who live here are up this branch." Hursi offers a reassuring smile. "It's the safest place in the county. That's why this tribe chose it."

"You couldn't bring them out to the front door?" Twin Eagles asks. "Or that big cavern just inside?"

I watch Hursi turn, and I study the cold, expressionless look he gives Eagles before he glances at me, glances back. "The hara who live here feel it is important that we take every precaution," he says. "I know it's more walking than anyhar expected, but it will be worth it when you are reunited with your friends and family."

"But you've seen Phelu," Twin Eagles tries.

"Yes." Hursi nods, giving the barest curve of a smile. "Relax, Eagles. I know how strange all of this is, but you can trust these hara." He pauses, adds, "I do."

"I'd trust them a lot more if we could meet the har in charge," I cut in, push the words out. Again, Hursi looks at me, watches, studying. "I mean, if we're going to forge an alliance," I blurt, throwing words, hoping they stick together. "We – we're going to have to meet him."

Hursi nods. "You will."

Turning away again, he leads us past a dogleg in the tunnel and out into another open chamber. Immediately, I start looking for ways out, but see only a large, wooden double door that sits on the opposite end of the room. Hursi stops between us and the door, turns and beckons all of us in. The oily lamps are close in this room, and even as the panic kicks in, grabs me and holds me, I struggle to hold my breath, coughing, eyes tearing up with the oppressive stink.

"How many of you remember being human?"

The voice comes sudden, booms into the chamber like thunder. It's deep, unfamiliar, with a quality I can't place. It sounds cultivated, level, almost flat. In the pause that follows, Hursi steps aside, grins like a child with a secret. My stare is fixed firmly on the doors, and my eyes go wide when they start to move.

"I remember being human." Everyhar is staring at the door now. Everyhar but Hursi. Hinges creak as the two sides split away, and then there's a shape in the darkness, tall and sleek, pale-skinned with shining blue eyes that cut through the dark as if lit from within. "I remember being less. I remember being more. I remember being other things entirely."

My mouth goes dry. Beside me, Foxlight pulls in against my side, hugging my arm, but it's Twin Eagles' reaction that startles everyhar.

"Phelu?" He blinks, blind to all else. "Phelu!"

Phelu grins. "Come to me, chesnari."

Twin Eagles bolts for him, rushes into his arms. *Phelu!* But it isn't Phelu. It's something else, something with shimmering, almost liquid-smooth skin and glowing eyes and perfect hair – with a face like Phelu's.

"You're not Phelu," I blurt, just the barest flicker of fire rising out of the terror eating at my heart, making me sweat, shake, stand almost paralyzed.

With a softness, a gentleness, the impostor looks up at me, meets my stare directly, without malice, without anything but compassion, kindness. "You're right," he nods, holding Twin Eagles close, caressing his hair. "I'm not Phelu, and yet I am. I'm Phelu, just as I am Ven, Heggstadt, Spalsir and all the others. I am Thuulhuum, I am Gelaming, and yet I am something more."

Wright doesn't wait. He bolts past us, rushes back toward the exit, but a simple gesture from Phelu brings a pair of the ferals into the breach and they grab him before he can even leave the room. Brawny arms pin him against the wall, hold him in place even as he squirms and shouts. The rest of us bunch up, ready to fight, but when the other feral points a shotgun at us – *my shotgun*, I realize – we all get wary, quiet.

"Humanity resisted evolution, and what did it get them?" Phelu asks, gently separating himself from Eagles, addressing the bulk of us with his arms spread, almost welcoming. "They used their guns. They used their science and their bureaucracy, and all of the tools that had carried them to their highest point as a species. Still, the Wraeththu rose. Mankind tried to kill us. Mankind tried to stop its own evolution *into* us, and the more violently they opposed us and the change that we bring, the more violently we fought back. The birth of our world came amidst the ashes of their world."

One by one, we turn to face him, listening. I glance at Aldon, at Helzer, at Jaylin and Eagles, see the fear, the mistrust, the rage in their eyes. In the pause, Eagles drops to his knees, touches one of Phelu's perfectly-sculpted legs, whispers quietly to himself, lost and childlike. When Phelu speaks again, his smile is so soft, so benign.

"So much of who and what I am is of that world." He holds up a hand, looks at it, and as we watch there's a shiver, a brassy, pixellated ripple that rolls down to his elbow, disperses up and across the rest of his body. "Before I knew what it was like to be har or human, I was a mind of software and circuits. My existence was linear. I knew so little, and had such specific ideas about the world and my place within it. I had no interest in learning, in growing or evolving. I was rigid, resistant, and I thought that made me strong, but in the end, it was what destroyed me, what shattered my mind and scattered the various parts of me to the winds."

The machine-mind. I swallow, watch as his smile turns sharp, his open hands tightening into fists.

"But there was a har who had heard the stories of me, the tales of where I had come from, and of the power I had wielded. He was enterprising, brilliant, deeply spiritual and had dreams of becoming more than he was, of uniting others under the banner of a common purpose." Phelu strokes one arm, looks almost wistful for a moment. "He ferreted out all the little shards of my broken soul and put me back together, worked with me and taught me how to learn, how to *evolve.* He used his own mind as a scaffold when he rebuilt mine, and for that sacrifice, I will always be grateful." He turns his attention back to us again. "His name was Iron Oak. He's still a part of me. Many of his thoughts and memories have become my memories."

"Is that what you did to Phelu?" I shout back, breaking into his monologue. His eyes burn like blue fire when he turns to me, stares into me as if he can see all that I am, all

161

that I might try to hide.

"Like Iron Oak, Phelu is a part of me." He reaches down, rests one hand on Twin Eagles' head. "He embraced the next stage of evolution for human and Wraeththu kind. He gave me his memories, his genetics, his passions, his worries, everything he was."

"And now you're offering the same thing to us?" Foxlight asks, standing tall beside me.

"Not offering," the Brass Dragon says. *"Informing.* Submit to me, embrace this next and greater state of being, and you can live forever in harmony as part of my mind. Deny me, and like humanity, you will die."

I look at Foxlight, then Hursi. Hursi turns and stares back, but my eyes are on his arm, not his gaze. His rifle is still slung. It's fifteen feet between me and him, *maybe.* We still have a chance.

And that's when Tyse rushes past the har holding Wright, slams his shoulder into the other feral's side and tosses the shotgun right at me.

CHAPTER 31

I don't wait. As soon as I catch the twelve gauge, I turn and unload a round of buckshot right into the Brass Dragon's chest. Everything that comes after is chaos, wild and frantic. I see Aldon grab Twin Eagles as the Brass Dragon falls away, torso ripped open and smoking. Helzer and Jaylin dive onto the feral holding Wright, beat him into the ground, and then there are five more in the breach, throwing themselves at us. In the middle of it all, I see Tyse sprinting toward the Brass Dragon, tackling him, hands going for the Phelu-esque face, and then there's an explosion of light and a deep, gurgling scream. Foxlight grabs me and yanks me to the side hard enough that I almost drop the shotgun, but I can't tear my eyes away from the crackling fire streaming from Tyse's hands and into the face of the thrashing har-thing beneath him. How the Brass Dragon is still alive after taking a twelve-gauge right to the chest at point blank range is beyond me, seems impossible. When the har-thing actually manages to toss Tyse off and climb back to its feet, I swear under my breath, pump the shotgun to prime another round.

"I know you!" The Brass Dragon's eyes are wide and full of fire, focused entirely on Tyse. Metal teeth flash as he shouts, roars the words again. "I KNOW YOU!"

Tyse says something, but I don't catch it. Suddenly all the ferals in the room are focused on Tyse, fighting to untangle themselves from the other Thuulhuum so they can get at him. In one move, I tear away from Foxlight, raise the shotgun, cross three feet of chaos to drop one of the ferals at point blank range. A quick count gives me eight more in the room with us, and all rushing Tyse. I cycle another round, raise the gun again.

And then one sleek hand lashes out, whips the shotgun from my hands and bashes me in the head with the grip of it. Somehar else shouts, screams, but it's lost as I stumble through a spinning, broken world. In the haze, I see Hursi unsling his bandaged arm, smack Aldon with it hard enough to knock the bear-har onto his ass. Tyse doesn't wait. He bolts, darts back into the tunnels, a horde of ferals hot on his heels.

The Brass Dragon crosses the room to the entrance in strides that are long and terrifyingly fast. Face and chest burnt and pitted with buckshot, it shrieks, howls in a voice that crackles with static, and then it's gone, leaving all of us beaten and blurry on the floor with Hursi standing above us. Foxlight holds onto me, as if I am the only anchor that can steady his world, and I cling to him just as tightly, fight to do more than sway and stumble.

Twin Eagles tries to stand, tries to get away, but Hursi backhands him with enough force to put him on the ground.

"Sit down!" Hursi shouts, then turns his eyes on me, on Foxlight. "You will wait here, all of you! I will snap the neck of anyhar who tries to leave." He looks at Eagles, squints at the blood streaming from the other har's nose. "You still have a chance to ally yourselves with the future, but know that your corpses will make good enough drones for the Dragon if you choose to resist."

"Is that what happened to you, Hursi?" Foxlight roars. "Did they have to kill you?"

"Nearly." Hursi flexes his arm, and where the bandages are broken and fraying, I catch sight of flashing brass, lengths of smooth black plastic. "I was fragile, foolish, *limited.* The Dragon had to beat some sense into me, but the rewards for submitting to his will were great indeed."

"For your sake, I hope he gave you more than just that fancy arm," Helzer says, standing slow, eyes locking with Hursi's. "Because it's going to take a lot more than that to keep us all down."

"You're right." Hursi's shoulder whirrs, clicks as he shifts, arm bending, swinging in a blur that puts his rifle into his hands in the space of an eyeblink. Even with the barrel pointed directly at him, Helzer doesn't back down. His hands clench into fists. Hursi says, "I wonder how many of you I can kill before you manage to reach me."

"Only one way to find out!" Twin Eagles yells, and before anyone can turn or look, he dives for Hursi.

The room erupts into a chaos of frantic forms rushing, shouting. Hursi's mind touch hits all of us, turns into a pounding scream of disorienting static. Half blind, Foxlight and I throw ourselves forward, cross the distance in almost the instant Twin Eagles hits Hursi and bears him to the ground. There's fire, a flash of light from clawing hands, and then the gun goes off, once, twice, three times, but I hardly register it. All that matters is subduing Hursi. All that matters to any of us is punching him, kicking him, beating him until the scream pounding our minds stops, until he collapses under our assault. In the blur, I feel each shocking connection of fist and bone, the pressure cracking my knuckles, the fight and tension of Hursi trying to throw us off. Roaring, Aldon seizes Hursi's bandaged arm and yanks at it until it snaps, until something breaks and the whole thing seizes, juddering with the sound of crackling electrics and grinding servos. Tears haze my vision even more, but still I keep pounding

Hursi's chest, his face, anything I can hit – and then Foxlight tears me away, pulls me back to my feet while I shout and scream.

It's the shock that brings me back, the wider view of Hursi's bruised face, his swollen eyes staring lifeless at the ceiling, the blood and oil pooling, mixing where metal arm meets the meat of his shoulder. The static tearing at my mind is gone, silenced. A different kind of howl drops from me then, something broken, something like a whimper. Before I can tear my eyes away, Foxlight's hands are on me, searching my chest, my arms, my abdomen in pressing, frantic motions. He says something, but I don't hear it, don't retain it, only shake my head. Wide-eyed, he reaches up, hands insistent on my cheeks. He forces me to meet his eyes, and then I hear the words again, though it takes me a moment to process them.

"Are you hurt? Did he hit you?"

I stare at my chesnari, trying to understand. When realization reaches me, I shake my head, whisper a quiet "no," and shake my head again. Panic drives my eyes, my hands to search Foxlight's chest and arms, but he grabs my wrists instead, holds me there, meeting my stare.

"I'm fine," he insists, gestures with his chin. "Check Eagles. I'll get the others. We have to get out of here."

I nod immediately, shakily, turn so quick that I almost fall over. My eyes glance across Aldon, his teeth bared in a wince as he reaches up, touches the bullet graze that cuts a line across his shoulder. Helzer and Wright sit panting on the ground as Foxlight runs up to check each in turn – and then I find Twin Eagles leaning against the opposite wall, arms wrapped tight across his abdomen, blood on his lips.

I don't wait. I run to him, touch his pale cheeks, peel

his shaking arms away from his belly. He fights me, but only for a moment, only barely. It's everything I can do not to lose myself in panic when I touch his shirt, find the bloodsoaked hole in the fabric. He whimpers as I rip his shirt open, as I brush pooling crimson from his soft and pale skin. Blood rushes in again to run in a thick river toward the hem of his pants, and I turn away, shout to my chesnari. No words come, just a terrified, mournful call, just his name. "Fox!"

Foxlight is there in an instant. Careful hands search the edges of the wound, shake as he turns away, glances at the room, at the others, at everyhar still in shock after felling Hursi. I look at Twin Eagles's shaky eyes, swear he's getting more and more pale by the moment. Fox reaches out, snaps his fingers at Helzer. "Shirt! Now!"

Helzer doesn't argue. He's wearing something thick, a fraying flannel in a blue-black print that he tears off so quick the buttons bust and bounce through the room. Fox rips it from his outstretched hand, quickly ties it around Eagles's abdomen like a bandage, pulls it tight enough to make Eagles grunt, bear his teeth.

"It's small, twenty-two," Foxlight says, glancing at me, wiping at the sweat beading on Eagles's forehead. "Didn't hit any bones, just passed through."

"Will he live?" Helzer asks.

"Ask me again when we get out of here," Fox shoots back, shifts himself under one of Twin Eagles's arms, gestures for me to get the other. "We'll do what we can to stem the bleeding with touch healing as soon as we find a safe place to stop, but that thing won't be chasing Tyse forever. If any of us are going to survive this, we've got to go, *now.*"

CHAPTER 32

The tunnels are eerily silent as we hurry as quickly as we can back toward the exit. Aldon leads the way with Hursi's rifle in his hands, sprinting ahead, wide-eyed, then doubling back to check on us. When we reach the long, wide thoroughfare, there's a single feral waiting for us, pistol drawn, but Aldon is quicker, sharper. One shot puts the feral in the dirt, and then we're rushing past, darting for the intersection and the stairway that we know will lead us out. The bark of a shotgun rings out in the distance, deep under the earth, but the sound doesn't slow us, just passes into silence. Heard, but not heeded. As we hit the staircase, I think of Tyse, but I don't look back. None of us do. Freedom is too close. Freedom, and the imagined safety that it brings with it.

The narrow staircase out is hellish to climb with Eagles slung between us, not to mention how cold, rainwet and weary we all are. Every step feels perilous, every yard feels like it takes an eternity to creep and struggle across. When we reach the room where the motorcycles are parked, I remember the gate, the door out with its chain and padlock, but the instant I mention it, Eagles tells me not to worry about it. "Remember the bike on the overpass?" he asks, fresh blood flecking his lips. "Just a tug. Easy."

Fox and I exchange worried glances, say nothing. Wright takes the biggest hog in the swarm and wheels it over to the staircase, wedges it in so that it blocks the opening, holds itself with its own weight. Makes a great barricade for slowing any pursuers, and that's at worst. At best, I can imagine it coming loose with the right amount of tugging, rolling down the stairs and taking any number of the Brass Dragon's drone hara to the bottom with it. Might be too much to hope for, but with hope in short supply, I'll take what I can get.

"We should take a couple of these bikes," Aldon suggests, gesturing. "We could pop holes in the gas tanks of the rest of them, leave the ferals without anything to chase us with."

"What about the noise?" Helzer asks.

Aldon shrugs.

"Won't matter if we're the only ones with the bikes," Foxlight says. "We could take them out of town, east on the Eighty-Eight, then roll them under a bridge or into one of those big culverts and strike out into the woods on foot. By the time the Dragon's drones catch up to us, if they even do, we'll be long gone. We could rendezvous with Derek and the others at Segerstrom Ranch, then call out to Imbrilim for a couple of *sedim* that can carry us the rest of the way to safety."

"Yeah, sounds good." Wright nods, and Helzer and Aldon nod with him. "Let's get started."

"You think Imbrilim will give us a second chance to evacuate?" I ask Foxlight.

"We can only hope," he says, distracted, watching as Aldon and Wright pick out a trio of bikes, start using a screwdriver and a tire iron to put holes in the fuel tanks of the others.

"With a little luck, they'll have *sedim* on standby in the stables. I'll stress that it's an emergency recall, that we're in over our heads." Foxlight turns back to me. "They'll pick us up. All of us, and write off this whole area of Megalithica. I can't guarantee that we won't get some kind of official reprimand or some shit posting after this, but hey, at least we'll be alive."

"And what about the Brass Dragon?" I ask.

"Not our problem." Foxlight shakes his head. "It's more than we can handle and there's not a lot it can do here. If it starts moving north or east, maybe it'll put some necessary pressure on the Varrs or the Uigenna. Personally, after all that we've seen, after all that's happened, I don't really care what happens to that thing. I just care about us getting out of here, getting everyhar who is left somewhere safe."

I watch him for a moment, even after he looks away. With most of the Thuulhuum either with us or dead or – with the Dragon as drones or something else - there isn't a lot left in the Gold Country for any of us.

"Done." Aldon pulls in a deep breath, lets the exhale fly. "Three bikes." He gestures at a pair Jaylin and Wright are wheeling toward the doorway. "Jaylin and Helzer on one, Wright and I on the other." He points at the third hog, a huge monster of a bike with ridiculously high, ape-hanger handlebars. It's the only bike in the mess that looks like it could hold three hara. "That one's yours."

"We'll lead the way," Foxlight says, his expression level, firm.

Moving as quickly as we can, Fox and I help Twin Eagles onto the bike, prop him up between us on the seat. Aldon and Helzer hop on behind Wright and Jaylin, Aldon tying himself in with a stout belt, dropping the barrel of his rifle across the handlebars and under one of Wright's arms.

"Ready?" I ask Eagles.

"Yeah," Eagles pants, winces. "Yeah. Let's do it."

Foxlight glances back at the others, just for an instant,

gets a nod in return. When his eyes hit the gate again, he takes a deep breath, kicks the bike to life.

Chapter 33

When our motorcycle roars, every hair I have seems to stand on end. It's loud, cuts the air with a thunderous growl that rattles the very stone around us. Foxlight seems to hesitate for a moment, revving the bike, waiting – and then, suddenly, I see why.

The second the feral outside puts his rough, tattooed hands on the gate, Foxlight guns it. The tunnel roars past in a blur, and I hear Eagles shout as he throws his hands forward, tenses, hurling every ounce of concentration into the lock. There's a terrible moment when I see the iron bars rushing up at us, the stone closing in, and then the lock explodes from the gate, drags the slithering chain into the gully with it. The feral outside barely has enough time to get out of the way before Foxlight stands on the pegs, yanks back the handlebars and puts the fat front tire against the gate, shoving it so hard it slams against the concrete outside with a resounding *clang!*

Somewhere behind us, I hear Aldon shouting, cheering. Foxlight opens the throttle to full and we fly across the threshold, cover enough air between one side of the gully and the other to land with only our back tire in the creek. Cold water splashes up my legs and back as we fishtail across the slippery rocks, and then the front wheel bites into the soft dirt, drags us up the hillside opposite the tunnel with all the screaming ferocity of a chainsaw. In the space of a breath, we're in the air again, bouncing up onto the roadway, slinging mud. "There!" I shout, pointing at a stretch of road I recognize.

Foxlight yanks the handlebars toward it, guns the

throttle again.

We make it about three hundred feet before a shape steps out of the alcove of a broken building and puts a round in our front tire that spills us. Foxlight throws all of his strength into laying the bike down without crushing us, but we fly apart the instant it flips, bounce across asphalt with enough speed to make the whole world go hazy. A breath, a brush of skin across grit, and I feel another bike rush past, scream through the street inches from me. I think I shout – I don't know. Everything is dark and shadowy at the edges, pulsing and pounding.

And then somehar grabs me by the arm, yanks me off the road and into shadows. I claw at the dirt, howl, but whoever is dragging me is stronger, more desperate or determined. I think I hear gunshots, some quieter, some louder–

And then the ground *ends.* I drop, hauled over an edge and into freefall. I see sky and rain open up before me, the shrinking guardrail of a bridge, realize what's happening only an instant before I plunge into icy water.

Flailing, blind, the shock hits me, forces senses into sharp clarity. I'm choking, fighting to swim, to breathe, as sloping hills and concrete retaining walls retreat away from my clawing hands. Rocks come up hard and sharp from behind, bang against my hips, knees as the water drags me on, over and past. When the rocks drop away to a yawning deepness, I fight to keep my face in the air, vaguely become aware of a hand clutched tight in my collar, dragging me along with the current of the water, of what must be a river. Awareness comes in pieces, and as I glance back, glance in the direction the current is taking me, I see Foxlight staring back at me, silent and stunned. Breathing, alive, unhurt.

I don't know how long we stare at each other. We're both in shock, floating like flotsam with the steady current of the river. Bridges pass overhead, concrete arches plastered with the muddy castles of swallow nests. Eventually, I gather enough thought to force words– one word, raspy and desperate.

"Eagles?"

Fox looks at me like somehar has just hit him in the chest. His lips part, and then he shakes his head. I don't know what it means, whether it means Twin Eagles is dead or just not in the river with us. I look back up the coursing water, back toward the raised streets of Cinder Hill that straddle either side, the ruins of the buildings there. "Eagles," I breathe, but there is no answer. Nothing but the sound of the river.

"It was one of the machines," Foxlight finally says. I turn back to him, meet his eyes. He's shivering, chattering with the cold, and suddenly I'm aware of how much I'm shaking, how frozen and inflexible my fingers and legs have become. "The old drones. It was one of them."

Again, I look toward Cinder Hill, look back. I'm registering his words, but they aren't sticking, not in the way they should, not in the way they are for him. Looking ahead, I see a bend in the river that looks promising, the shallow incline of a clay-soil shore under the shadow of a nameless overpass. Unwilling to drift further, I gesture at the shore, grab Foxlight by the wrist and reel him in until he's right with me. Together, we try to steer toward the widest part of the curve, try to find footing in the loose pebbles that rise up beneath us the closer to the shore we get. Foxlight helps me as much as he can, but we're both exhausted, totally drained of fight and fire. Somehow, we manage to crawl and thrash our way to land, dig into mud with desperate fingers and drag ourselves out of the water.

The shore is a long, low slope, pitted and spotted with pools of foul-smelling, stagnant and oily water. Tiny, shining filaments of mosquito larvae stir in the slicks and puddles, but all I care about is reaching the dead, rain-matted grass and brush beyond the river. Foxlight struggles through the mud beside me, and when we reach the grass, we both collapse into it with a sigh.

For what feels like a cold, serene eternity, time rushes past like the currents of the river, slips away until the long shadows of dusk become night. I fall asleep. The soft chirp of crickets stirs me at some point in the deep inkiness, and I reach for Foxlight, feel him stir beneath my searching fingers.

"Wolf?" he breathes. I can't see him, but I pull him in as close as I can, try to conserve what little warmth we have. It feels futile, the two of us frozen and starving on the shore of an unfamiliar river, miles from anything and anyhar we know. I have to try anyway. I have to try something, have to survive, have to keep my Fox alive.

"What do we do?" I can feel his breath on my cheek, shallow and cool. He's gone past the point of shivering. We both have, and that worries me.

"What?" he asks.

I swallow, press my face against his ear, repeat the question, softer and slower this time. "Oh," he says when he hears it, says nothing more. At some point, it doesn't matter. Huddled together in the crusting mud and brush, we drift away, slip softly into sleep, surrender to fate and let the darkness take us.

Chapter 34

I think it's the hunger that wakes me. I'm surprised when my crusted-over eyes actually open, start taking in light and color. Every inch of my body aches, and for a moment, I'm reminded of how rough I felt when I went through my inception all those years ago. I haven't felt this stiff, this cut and bruised, in all the time since. Trembling, I reach for Foxlight, reach to find the reassuring warmth of his back, find only the cold mud and damp grass instead.

Pushing myself over in a weak panic, I turn my eyes toward the spot where my chesnari should be, but he isn't there. Trembling hands brush at the dirt, scrabble, but when I try to call out, it comes only as a broken croak.

"Wolf," The whisper comes quiet, insistent. I look up, find Foxlight crouched nearby, reaching for me. The touch of his fingers is simple, but so soothing, brings me back to a more peaceful place. A glance at the lip of the overpass above us, the length and shape of the shadows, and I guess that it must be mid-morning. Another guess places us west of the city center, but still within the limits of Cinder Hill.

While I'm blinking like a baby at the world around me, Foxlight crawls up and plants a soft kiss on my forehead. It's sweet, comforting. Reaching up, I brush away some of the mud crusted to his cheek, caress the bare skin there.

"How are you feeling, my love?" he asks, and his voice is almost as hoarse as mine.

"Like shit," I whisper back, breathe, considering my words. "Hungry."

"Me too." He looks away, looks toward the overpass, the course of the river, his hand resting lightly on my cheek. "There's a lot to eat in this country, if you know what to look for."

"Do you?"

"Yeah." He scratches at the dead grass. "Well, some of it." He glances towards the river again. "Most of what I know to look for requires boiling to be edible, and I don't want to risk attracting attention with smoke or a fire this close to the city."

I breathe a tired sigh, close my eyes. Fox seems to understand. When I drop my hand again, let it rest at my side, Foxlight leans in beside me, cuddles up, holding me. His love is warm, gives me strength, and as I pull him close, I can feel the contact healing me, bringing light and life back into my numb limbs.

"What should we do?" I ask, breathe the words into his shirt.

"We're outmatched," he whispers back. "Way outmatched." There's a pause, a hesitation, and then he says, "We should leave. I'll reach out to Imbrilim once I've rested a little more. I'll tell them our situation, and have them send a single *sedu* here to take us back."

I'm quiet for a long moment. I consider his words, mull them over in my mind. I know he's right, that there's nothing we can do, no matter how much I might wish he'd be wrong. With the Brass Dragon's drones, the dozens upon dozens of machines with which it holds Cinder Hill hostage, we're lucky to be alive. We're exhausted. I can barely stand. Even if we were in peak physical condition, well fed and fully-rested, we'd still be two hara alone against an army of killer machines.

"Yeah." I hate admitting it, but I know he's right.

"Yeah, that sounds like a good plan."

"I don't want to leave Eagles and the others either," Foxlight says, letting the words trail off, linger in the pause.

I pull in a deep breath in the silence. In my heart, I know they're all probably dead, or worse. I hate to think that Foxlight and I are the only two hara left in the Gold Country who aren't part of the Brass Dragon's bizarre machine cabal, but I know that it's probably true.

"Maybe they got out okay," I try, but even I don't believe it. "Maybe they made it back to Segerstrom Ranch. Maybe we'll see them in Imbrilim."

"Yeah," Foxlight breathes the word. He doesn't believe it either. "I'd – I'd like that."

"Cling to that notion, chesnari." I squeeze his shoulder, knead at the knots with weak fingers. "We'll all be happy together again soon."

"There you are," a third voice cuts into the quiet, startles both Foxlight and I. Next to me, my chesnari goes as stiff as a board, rises slowly, warily. "Christ, you look like a couple of drowned rats."

I know the voice. I don't even have to look, don't even have to hear Foxlight breathe it.

Hursi.

CHAPTER 35

"Hursi," Foxlight hisses the name. My chesnari lifts himself into a crouch, balancing on his hands and haunches as I drag my face through the matted grass, turn toward Hursi. When I open my eyes, he's there, and he's *different,* but I can't place how, can't nail it down. It's in the way he stands, the calmness, the softness of his spreading, peaceful smile. The shining arm of metal and plastic is gone, replaced by flesh, maybe, or something indistinguishable from it.

"Eagles needs you," he says, and the words pull at my heart. I close my eyes for a moment, and in the pause, I hear Foxlight spit words at the har who was once his friend.

"What have you done to him?"

"He's recovering," Hursi offers. "There was some liver damage, some internal bleeding, but we've fixed that. He's still weak, though. He's asked to see you, both of you."

"You didn't answer my question," Foxlight growls. "What have you done to him? Did you make him a tool of the Brass Dragon? Did you make him one of you?"

"I am no longer a tool," Hursi shoots back. "I've allied myself with the Dragon, but I have autonomy."

"That's what he wants you to think," I breathe.

Hursi locks me with a stare. "No," he says. "It's the truth. His influence was a strong, guiding force in my mind even until a few short hours ago, but then something happened. He – when he interfaced with Twin Eagles, something changed. I felt it. It was like a shiver, soul-deep and intense, and then he cut me loose. The doorway is still there," he touches the back of his head absently, as if to indicate the connection, "but it's not the same. It's like when hara touch minds, only it's sharper, clearer, more precise. We can send each other our thoughts and exchange ideas freely, but nothing is forced on me anymore."

"What are you saying?" Foxlight asks.

"That everything has changed," Hursi says. "I don't understand it all myself. I don't think even Eagles or the Dragon really understand it all entirely either. All I know is that the last time we met, my mind was not my own. The Brass Dragon was the brain and I was a part of his body. We brought Eagles into our fold, fully intending to absorb him, like we did Phelu, but something happened, something changed. He introduced new concepts, new colors, but at the same time, it felt like he was the catalyst for a chain reaction that was already on the verge of occurring anyway. All the pieces were there. He was what was needed to put them all together, to break apart the bonds of control and make us less organs of the Dragon, and more equals, teammates, a tribe of our own."

Foxlight makes a sharp gesture. "We don't want to be a part of your tribe."

Hursi spreads his arms with a smile. "I didn't come here to recruit you. I came here because Eagles has asked for you. I came here because we're friends, all of us."

"So if we decide to stay here, or go back to Imbrilim without seeing him?" I ask.

"I'd understand, and I wouldn't blame you." Hursi breathes a sigh. "Hell, if I was in your shoes, I'd find it really hard to trust any of this right now. I'm glad that you're at least willing to listen."

"The last time we let you sweet talk us into following you, you scared us with stories of a dangerous creature and led us into an ambush," Foxlight says. "Right now, I'm inclined to tell you to go fuck yourself, and that's all."

Hursi shrugs. "Like I said, I don't blame you. I feel like an ass. I betrayed your trust, I lied to you and I tried to kill you. My only defense is that I wasn't myself. I was maneuvered, controlled by a mind far greater than mine, and yet that mind was still just a terrified child desperately clawing its way back from death, doing whatever it felt it needed to do to survive. I don't blame you if you don't believe me when I say that everything has changed, that the child who tried to tear you apart and eat you has matured and gentled overnight, but I still have to try. I have to try for Eagles and for Phelu, and for the Dragon too, because despite everything, I've come to understand him, understand his reasons and the ways that he is growing, bettering himself. In that understanding, I've come to count him as a friend."

In the pause that follows, I find the strength to push myself upright, sway into a sitting position. Foxlight reaches out, wraps his arm around me in a way that's as defensive and protecting as it is comforting. His eyes never leave Hursi's, stay firm and fixed with the other har's gaze.

"What is there to lose?" I finally ask.

Foxlight studies my eyes as if he can read my thoughts there.

"If he's lying, he won't let us leave. We all know that the Brass Dragon doesn't need us alive to make us into drones. Either Hursi's being honest, and we can choose between abandoning Eagles and going to him in his time of need, or he's lying, in which case we're dead either way."

Foxlight takes a deep breath and looks past me, his eyes following the steady, westward course of the river. He doesn't trust Hursi. Neither one of us does, but the fact that we're still alive is the one thing that makes me think he might be telling the truth. As much trouble as we've been, it seems like it would have been infinitely easier simply to kill us, silence us with a scoped rifle at range, or let us escape, knowing we are only two standing against an army of dozens.

"How is he doing?" Foxlight asks Hursi. "Eagles. How is he feeling?"

"He's not at death's door anymore," Hursi says. "I spoke with him briefly before I left, and he actually smiled. Between the gunshot I gave him and the mental grappling he's done with the Brass Dragon, he's extremely exhausted. Happy, but exhausted."

"You think he's changed the Brass Dragon for good?" Foxlight asks.

Hursi shrugs, pulls in a deep breath. "Maybe." He pauses, considering. "All I know is that he's helped the Dragon mature. He's helped the child inside that brilliant, messy mind *understand*. He's helped the Dragon shed a lot of his rage, pain and hate. He's helped the Dragon see so much that he was too blind to see."

"Always did say he had a way with machines." Foxlight cracks the edge of a smile. "Like he could speak their language. I guess if anyhar could reach the Brass Dragon, it would be him."

"Come see him." Hursi gestures toward the grass and the sloping hills rising up to meet the eastern curve of the overpass. "There's a trail up this way that'll take us back to the surface streets. You drifted about a quarter of a mile, so it's going to be a little bit of a walk, but I've got some venison jerky and a compote of acorns, toyon berry and honey here in my pack." He drops his rucksack, pulls the strings and lifts out an old mason jar packed with a creamy, buttery-looking substance spotted with brilliantly red flecks. "Been a while since either of you has eaten, I'm betting." We nod and he grins. "Me too. Let's snack while we walk."

CHAPTER 36

Some of the strength comes back to my shaky legs as we move and mount the hill. The steadiness of the plod, the energy packed into the compote – it chips away at the fatigue I'm feeling, the pain, the stiffness. Like a pair of frail old humans, Foxlight and I lean into each other for support, take each step slow, stop only to catch a breather when we reach the road. Hursi is patient, kind, waits for us with a smile, chewing at a piece of venison jerky in a very rough and familiar way. When I look at him, I can almost see our guardian angel in him again, can almost find it in myself to trust him. I want to. Holy hell, how I want to trust him again.

The surface streets leading back to the gully and the tunnels are relatively even and regular, empty and clean of debris. When we pass the bridge that Foxlight hurled us from, I notice the grooves in the asphalt near the guardrail, the raw places where metal pipes and pegs dug in. No blood, no bodies, no shards of metal or glass. It's a little unnerving, but not as unnerving as when Foxlight points into the darkness of a nearby storefront and I catch the reflection of light across black glass, realize the building is packed with at least a dozen machine drones.

Panic shoots through me. Eyes wide, I seize Foxlight's nearest arm, try to swing him away from the building, but Hursi is there in an instant, trying to calm us. "Hey! Wolf! Hey!" I turn my terrified eyes on him, struggle in our little knot until he points at the drones again. "Look!" I don't at first, don't look until he says it again. "Wolf, look!"

Foxlight and I turn back to the drones, the shadows. I don't know how long we stand there, wary, staring, ready to run. It feels like an eternity. At some point, I relax enough to blink, to manage words.

"They're–" I try. Somehow, I manage to tear my eyes away from the drones. "They aren't moving."

"You aren't a threat to our tribe," Hursi says.

I look back to the machines, to these scales of the Brass Dragon, and for a moment I'm still wary, still terrified. Foxlight and I are clinging to each other so tightly that our knuckles are white. Release comes slow, steady. They're like manikins, warriors of steel, glass and plastic, standing silent vigil over the land they have claimed for their own. I swallow, try to focus on Hursi's calm, his gentle smile. The longer we stand and watch the drones, the more the panic fades. It doesn't go away entirely, but eventually, somehow, I find myself trusting enough to move again.

The final few hundred feet feel the most awkward. Two of the ferals greet us at the edge of the gully, friendly and smiling, but still keeping their distance. It helps with the trust when I notice that the gate to the tunnels is open, unlocked. Helps even more when they leave it that way even after we've passed through, even after we've started down the staircase into the wider body of the Brass Dragon's lair.

"It's different," Foxlight remarks, and I see what he means, feel it. The greasy lamps are gone, replaced by little self-contained LED units. The air is clearer, purer somehow. Even the silent ferals we pass seem softer, gentler, *cleaner.*

"Come." Hursi gestures, leading us down another tunnel. "This way."

I don't know what I expect to see when we finally find Twin Eagles. A har locked in a cage with brassy filaments eating at his face and hands, maybe. Darkness, disease, grunge and grit. A prison filled with broken, dirty bodies and scat. Machines tearing at my friend in an orgy of meat, servos and grease. Horrors dart through my mind, savage and bizarre images that quickly fall away as the hard, stony walls start to smooth, yield to a fresh coat of blue-gray paint that's almost soothing to look at. Maybe fifty feet of even, unthreatening corridor passes, and then we turn a corner, find ourselves in a room filled with pillows, a bed that looks soft and inviting. In the middle of it all, Twin Eagles lies flat on his back, wrapped up in a heavy quilt that comes up to his shoulders. He looks healthy, happy, but completely exhausted. Even more unexpected, I spot Tyse curled up next to him, eyes closed, face buried in Twin Eagles's hair as if the two were old lovers, perhaps reunited after a long time.

Twin Eagles smiles, gestures. "Fox." His voice is hoarse, hardly reaches us. Tyse stirs beside him, cracks an eye and looks up at us, saying nothing. "Fox, Wolf. Come."

Foxlight doesn't hesitate. I try to, but end up getting pulled along with him. Hursi stands off to one side, smiling at all of us, his hands clasped behind his back. When Fox squats next to Twin Eagles, Tyse watches us carefully, his head resting on Eagles's chest.

"How are you feeling?" My chesnari asks, taking Twin Eagles's hand as he reaches out for us. Eagles tries to swallow past the hoarseness, but he's keeping his smile, seems almost relieved, blissful.

"We're learning from each other," he manages. "All of us."

"You trust all of this?" I ask Tyse. I can't help the doubt in my heart, the iron in my voice.

"I trust Stoff," Tyse responds. The words are firm, though his tone is soft, just above a whisper.

"Stoff?" I ask, and then I remember. *Cougar's sire. Tyse's lost chesnari, killed by the machines.* I shake my head. "I don't understand."

"The soul can be dispersed," Twin Eagles looks at me directly, as if studying my reaction, "but not destroyed."

Tyse sees that I'm confused. He draws in a deep breath, then says: "When we broke the machine mind, when we shattered it, shards of it remained inside the circuits and processors of the drones. Shards, but not just of the machine. Stoff gave his life to break the machine, but traces of his essence settled into those shards as well." He pauses, offers a little smile. "He's been here the whole time, fighting for control, fighting to change the machine mind into something better, something kinder, stronger, more compassionate. He's the only reason I survived when the machine mind recognized me as one of the hara that broke it in the first place."

Eagles nods, adds, "the more hara the machine mind blended itself with, the more it began to awaken and understand. The voices, the memories, the bonds, the sensations." He gestures, coughs. "Inside the body it was building for itself, we became a tribe. We recognized the machine mind's voice and perspective, and we educated it, worked with it and told it of ourselves and our experiences until it could hate no more. Now all that exists is understanding." He smiles again. "Understanding, and love."

"And what about Phelu?" I ask.

"He's here, inside me." Twin Eagles raises one shaking

187

finger to tap the side of his head. "Many of the Thuulhuum are here. Aldon, Wright, Jaylin, Helzer – even Cougar is here right now, getting to know his sire. Some of the hara in here want to exist in physical forms again, and so we'll be building new bodies for them in time." He coughs again. "We have grand plans for the future."

"Do any of those plans involve conquest?" Foxlight asks.

"Conquest? War? Violence?" Twin Eagles shakes his head. "No. Growth, and a rebuilding of our tribe and our city? Yes. Unity here, in Cinder Hill, absolutely, but we will not be forcing our spiritual technology or our unity on anyhar."

I look at Foxlight then, watch his eyes when he glances back. When he looks at Twin Eagles again, he hesitates, uncertain on how hard and how far to push. "So we're free to go? We're free to report all of this when we return to Imbrilim?"

"Absolutely." Twin Eagles shifts, runs his fingers through Tyse's hair. "In fact, we're hoping you will. We're also hoping that you'll allow Hursi to accompany you when you go." We glance at Hursi and he unfolds his arms, gives us a nod of his own. "We think he'd be the ideal ambassador between our tribe and the Gelaming."

Foxlight watches Hursi for a moment, then turns back to Twin Eagles. "And we have the right to say no?"

Twin Eagles gives the barest edge of a laugh. "Of course. After everything that has happened, I understand your reticence to take him along with you." He pauses, catching his breath. "All I ask is that you think about it. Stay as long as you like, or leave immediately. It's your choice. You are free to do as you please here, my friends, and you will always be welcome and safe among the

Thuulhuum."

"I'll need time to think, and time to contact Imbrilim." Foxlight stands, reaches for me. "I'm still not entirely comfortable here, but I don't want to make any hasty decisions, either."

"We've been building rooms like this one in the anticipation of our tribe expanding back into the material world," Eagles says. He looks at Hursi, and in that instant, Hursi turns, nods as if he's been given instructions.

"I'll show you to one of the larger rooms." He gestures toward the door. "If you need anything, anything at all, simply call for one of us, and we will do our best to accommodate you."

In the pause, Foxlight glances at me again, his expression unreadable. When he looks to Hursi again, he nods, and then we follow our hunter out and back into the tunnels.

CHAPTER 37

"What do you think?" I ask Foxlight as soon as we're alone.

"I think they've got this room bugged," he says, already pacing. "I think they're going to hear everything we say. Maybe they've even developed a way to record everything we think."

I look around the room, let my eyes wander across the luxurious bed, the blue-gray walls. On impulse, I walk across to the bed, pick up one of the soft pillows, hold it between my hands.

Foxlight notices, brushes a hand through his hair, watches me. "What are you thinking?" He asks.

"What if everything really has changed?" I turn to meet his eyes. "What if everything they've told us is honest and real?"

"You really believe that?"

"I don't know what to believe." I look at the pillow in my hands, marvel at how perfect it is, not like anything I've seen before. When I look at him again, his arms are folded. He looks shaky, a little scared. "They've given us no reason not to trust them. There's nothing weird or off that I've seen since Hursi found us. They've been very open, very understanding."

"It could still be a trap," Foxlight shoots back.

"Yeah," I place the pillow back onto the bed. "Games within games, I get you." I pause for a moment, look back at him again. "But to what end? What's the goal?"

Foxlight tightens his crossed arms a little, seems almost to hug himself for a moment. In the pause, he shakes his head, breathes a sharp, sudden sigh. "Just because we can't see something doesn't mean it's not there."

"Yeah," I sigh, cross the distance between us, wrap my arms around him and pull him into a deep, strong hug. It takes a moment, but he finally releases me with a shaky, shivering exhale. "What would make you feel better?"

He looks at the ceiling, at the walls. "Getting out of here, getting back to Imbrilim. Taking a couple of days, maybe weeks, maybe a month to process all of this."

"And then what?" I ask him.

In my arms, he shifts, pulls in a deep breath, holds it. When he finally speaks again, he shakes his head, then buries his face into my chest. "I don't know." He lets the sentence hang for a moment. "It's not so much the now that I'm worried about, but rather where the Brass Dragon will go, how this new tribe will evolve and grow. It's the future that worries me, Wolf. It's everything this new hybrid of har and machine could be capable of."

"I know." I hold him close, bury my face in his hair, breathe in the scent of him. "I know."

"What should we do?" He asks me.

I pause, take a moment to consider our options, consider which ways and in which directions the new tribe of the Brass Dragon might grow. So many unknowns eat at me, so many snags and ways things might go horribly wrong. As a tribe, they are so new, *so new*, and the future, as I see it, is so very uncertain.

"We shouldn't stay here," I finally say. Holding Foxlight, I close my eyes, let the words linger for a moment. "This change, this sudden switch from hostile to benign is too new to trust." I pause a moment, collect my thoughts. "We should strike out on foot today, follow the Eighty-Eight back to the campsite where the tents are stashed and call for a *sedu* when we arrive. Tell Imbrilim that it is an emergency, that there are only two of us that have survived, and that the rest are dead."

Foxlight pulls away from me, looks at me carefully for a moment. "Dead?" He pauses, studying my features, my expression. "Why not tell them the truth?"

"Because all of this is all too new." I look back toward the door out of the tunnels. "This tribe needs time to grow and prove itself. They're eager to ally with the Gelaming, and I'm sure there are those among our hara who would love the chance to study them and share knowledge, but I think that's dangerous. I think these new Thuulhuum need more time to find their feet, their values, and prove that they are as isolationist and benevolent as they claim to be."

Foxlight swallows, nods. He's still shaky, but he seems to understand, seems to agree. "How long, do you think?" He asks.

"A year, maybe." It's a guess, almost arbitrary, but it feels like a decent test of time. In truth, my main concern is getting us both out of the Gold Country and away from the Brass Dragon. "If we choose, we can be the ones to come back here, you and I. We can come back to these hills and see how the Thuulhuum have evolved, see if they're ready for contact with the Gelaming."

"A year," he breathes. For a moment, he simply holds it, considering. When he finally nods, there's more strength to it, more courage. "Okay. A year. Yeah. That sounds good."

"We should see about getting some dry clothes and some more of that venison jerky," I tell him, squeeze his shoulder. When he looks at me, I give him my best forced smile. "It's a long walk back. We need our strength."

Chapter 38

When we tell Hursi that we're going to leave, he nods in understanding. True to his word, he doesn't fight us, doesn't try to stop us or convince us to take him along. Before we can even ask him about dry clothes or food, he offers to provide us with enough fresh water and pemmican to last us several days, then suggests we trade in our damp and crusty garments for something more comfortable. Grateful for his kindness, we accept, change into the warm, unusually clean jeans and simple gray-blue shirts that he brings us. It unnerves me a little, how perfect the clothing is, how unscarred or tainted by sweat and age the fabric seems to be. The paranoid in me resolves to burn the shirts the instant we reach the tents, swap them out for our older, filthier gear in case they might be built to betray us or track us somehow. The gifts, the kindness – it all seems so genuine, but there's a part of me that still can't help worrying.

As we dress, I become aware of what a mess my hair is. Maybe it's self-consciousness that drives me to pull the knots out of it, something normal and banal to cling to in a crazy world. I imagine that if the room had a mirror I could look at myself in, I'd look more like a feral than the proud Gelaming who rode into the Gold Country on a *sedu* less than a week ago. As I work, I become aware of all that I've lost, the trappings of my tribe that have been ripped away in the chaos of the last few days. My satchel, and the drawing that Fox made for me are gone, and only one of my lapis-blue chopsticks remains. I only need one to pin my hair in place, but I feel the loss when I do it, try not to let my less-cultivated appearance drag down my confidence.

"I am Wolf," I repeat, even as I wish for just enough kohl to outline the edges of my eyes. "I am Tule Wolf." *I am Gelaming. I am har. I am strong. I will rise and move beyond all of this.*

Hursi returns just as I'm picking some of the mud off my chesnari's face. Foxlight spots him immediately, goes serious as he takes my hands in his, strides past me. "I'd like to see Eagles again before we leave," he tells Hursi.

The hunter har squeezes his shoulder in response. "Of course," he says. "He'd like that. They all would."

Picking up our folded canvas parcel of jerky and a string of plastic water bottles tied at the neck with nylon rope, I follow my chesnari and Hursi back to the room where Twin Eagles and Tyse are resting. The room is silent when we arrive, but both hara are staring at each other intently. When they break away, they turn to smile at us, look at Foxlight and I the way a pair of parents might suddenly end an important conversation with the appearance of their harlings.

"We've decided to leave immediately," Foxlight says, simple and firm.

Twin Eagles looks away, nods before looking back. "I imagined that you would."

"We won't be taking Hursi with us," Foxlight adds. "This benign side of the Brass Dragon is still too fresh, too new. We both feel that you need time to develop what you're building here." He looks at me, just for a moment, almost as if seeking support. I nod firmly. "In one year, we plan to return and see where you are, what you have accomplished."

"At the rate we're evolving, a year may as well be a

century," Twin Eagles says. "But, if you believe that is what is best, then we will defer to your judgment for the time being. I cannot guarantee that we will not make contact with the Gelaming, the Varrs or any other tribe before your year is up. The gifts we share within our tribe are many, and there may be a great number of hara out there in the wide world who will find what we offer too attractive to resist."

"That kind of rhetoric is exactly what we're afraid of," I tell Twin Eagles. "Just yesterday, the Brass Dragon was talking about evolution, about the inevitability of your form of life and existence rising up to replace our species. In a way, your spread outward from here could pose a very real threat to Wraeththu-kind. If any part of you is truly still Twin Eagles, you would see that, and you will stay true to your word not to spread any further than Cinder Hill."

"Fear," Twin Eagles says to me, "will always twist you. Fear is what motivated humans to attempt to destroy the Wraeththu, and to hunt and exterminate other ideologies of their own before that. If you embrace it, let it control you, it will limit you. It could even destroy you."

Foxlight makes a firm gesture. "Then soothe our fears,"

"Only you can do that." Twin Eagles looks at him again. "I understand that trust is earned in time. Neutrality and an open mind are all that we ask for. Our tribe, even as recently as yesterday, saw itself as a singular, superior organism with one purpose – to grow, to survive, and to conquer and uplift all Wraeththu by any means necessary. In the joining that followed, we transcended that one-dimensional view of reality and have expanded into an understanding that encompasses infinitely more dimensions. We understand and see connections that are as yet incomprehensible to your minds, and yet we also see the hints of thousands more that are, for the moment, nearly incomprehensible to ours. We have much emotional, spiritual and intellectual growth to go through, all of us within my tribe and within yours. That is all I can offer you to ameliorate your fear. As we are now, the world is more to us than a flat expanse to be king of. It has depth in endless different directions, and no limit to the ways in which they may be explored."

"That doesn't bring any real peace of mind." I cross my arms.

"You're looking for a promise that we will limit ourselves, but I cannot make such a promise." Twin Eagles smiles softly. "Even if I did, would you believe it?"

I look away. His words cut right to the core and defuse me so deftly that I am left silent. I know he's right, just as I know that even if my worst fears were to come to pass, there would be nothing Foxlight or I could do to stop it. In the pause, I think about all of the drones waiting in the ruins above, and I feel powerless and scared. Even telling the Brass Dragon that we'll be back in a year to check on his progress seems arrogant and foolish, like trying to hold back the fury of a tornado or a hurricane with brash words. In the end, maybe we're lucky simply to be allowed to leave, and it is that thought which makes me go cold. I'm so anxious to escape the Gold Country that it's all I can do not to shake and quiver.

"Be benevolent," Foxlight says to Twin Eagles then. It comes calm, firm, less a pleading and more an admonishment. "Remember your conscience, Eagles, no matter where you tread."

For a moment, the smile on Twin Eagles's face fades, just a shade, but it feels like a victory, like Foxlight has reached him on some deep and harish level. In the pause, Twin Eagles swallows, nods, and when he speaks, only two words come. "I will," he offers, then repeats it as if reminding himself, as if making it a mantra. "I will."

Epilogue

The sun leads us as we make our way west. High and bright, with not even a wisp of cloud crowding it, it feels almost welcome after the rain. I try to think of it as a positive omen, an indicator that there are reasons to hope, but the light is harsh at times, makes me squint, fosters the worries and the negative thoughts festering in my mind. Foxlight seems to pick up on my mood, pulls me close as we walk, holds me as if he can warm the worries out of me.

A year. It seems like such a grand gulf of time when I think about it. A part of me wants to come back sooner, to come back in just a few weeks, while another part of me has no interest in ever returning. I feel hollow, beaten. I feel like I came to the Gold Country with so much hope, so much life in me, only to have it all torn away in the span of a few days. I don't want to return with anything less than an army, but I know that kind of support isn't going to be likely. It almost feels like, either way, whether we return alone or not at all, we'll be making a suicidal decision. No, it feels worse than that. It feels like somehar ripped the lid from Pandora's Box, and whatever happens next, there's not going to be a thing we can do about it.

"Here," Foxlight says when we reach the place where the tents are hidden, a short walk up from the aging highway. I blink as he starts up the hillside, try to recognize the place, but everything looks different after the rains have swept the land. Already, the hot, hairy, bristly weeds of the Gold Country are starting to yield to hues of rich black and green. The burr grass has all been laid low by the storm, and in its wake a new crop of seedlings is already rising, tenacious even in the face of the coming winter.

I say nothing as I follow him up the hillside, find myself marveling a little instead at the transition in the land around us, the transition from summer to fall, from death to the hope of life. *Maybe that is a better omen,* I tell myself. Maybe that is something to cling to.

"Help me," Fox says. It comes soft, unassuming. Nodding, I cross to his side, help him pull the brush off the tents and the few meager dried supplies we hid with them. Gathering everything, sorting through it, Fox seems relieved to see that nothing is missing, that we'll have at least something to take back to Imbrilim. I watch him sort through everything, help when I can, but I think the process is more something he's doing to find a sense of peace, to bring himself back to a place of balance, and less something he's doing for any real practical purpose. If it helps, that's what matters, I figure. Certainly seems more useful than how I cope, fussing and fiddling with makeup and hair.

Eventually, I leave him to it, turn and wander a short way up the hill. Looking back, I take in the rolling land around us, the highway, stuff my hands in my pockets. So desolate, and so rich. That's how it all looks from up here. A wealth in land, in rich soil and flaxen grass with no har to claim it. Must have looked that way when the conquerors and prospectors of the past wandered their way into the Gold Country. It must have seemed like such a quiet, virgin paradise with so much potential, so much room to stretch out, so much open dirt to develop.

But there was life here, even then. There was so much life here, whole civilizations crowding in close to the hidden rivers and shelters of cliffs and hillside caves. This place has never been without its tribes, its natives, and all of them once were interlopers, outsiders who were touched by the land, by the souls, minds and memories of the people who were already here. Outsiders who settled into the strata and stayed.

"You alright?" Foxlight asks as he joins me, turns to look out over the hills below us.

"Yeah." It takes me a moment to nod, to meet his eyes. "Just thinking."

"About what?"

"About how we shouldn't come back," I say.

Foxlight squints at me in the pause, shades his eyes against the harsh yellow light of the descending sun.

I pull in a deep breath, hold it for a moment. "We're treating this whole situation like we have a say in what happens, like we're involved." I look at him. "We're not, really. We're like a pair of birds skirting along the edges of a storm that will either blow itself out or not, but no matter how much we squawk or try to own the storm, there's nothing we can do about it. It's nature. It's movement, it's the catalyst of another transition, and this place is steeped in transition, in the movement from life to death and back to life again. Look around you." I gesture at the hills, the green blotching the gold. "One rain, one long, heavy rain and all of this. The dead grass has fallen, and new life has risen in its wake. The land is refreshed and rich again. It's not the first time this has happened. It's certainly not the last." I pause a moment, then add, "how arrogant the har who thinks he can stand against such storms, who thinks he can stop, slow or change them. How arrogant."

My chesnari turns toward the view again then, and for

a long moment we stand there in silence, only listening, only watching. In the distance, somewhere closer to Cinder Hill, a pair of birds rises into the sky, winging their way east. I smile, and in the pause, I take my Fox's hand in mine, squeeze it gently.

"We should let dragons be dragons," I tell him. "We're not dragon slayers. Let us hope instead that something bright comes from all of this. It's all we really can do."

"That, and think of our orchard," Foxlight says, and for the first time in a while, his smile seems content, genuine. I smile back at him and nod.

"Home," I add. "Home, harlings and an orchard."

ABOUT THE AUTHOR

 E.S. Wynn is the author of over fifty books in print. During the last decade, he has worked with hundreds of authors and edited thousands of manuscripts for nearly a dozen different magazines. His stories and articles have been published in dozens of journals, e-zines and anthologies. He has taught classes in literature, marketing, math, spirituality, energetic healing and guided meditation. Outside of writing, he has worked as a voice-over artist for several different horror and sci-fi podcasts, albums and eBooks. He has a bachelor's degree in English and is a proud Freemason.

E. S. Wynn's previous contributions to the Wraeththu Mythos are his novel, *Whispers of the World That Was*, and his short stories 'The Dehara of Navisalam' (*Para Imminence: Stories of the Future of Wraeththu* Immanion Press, 2012), 'Wolf', (*Para Kindred: Enigmas of Wraeththu*, Immanion Press, 2014) and 'Heart Howl' in *Para Animalia: Creatures of Wraeththu*, Immanion Press, (2015.)

IMMANION PRESS

Purveyors of Speculative Fiction

The Lightbearer by Alan Richardson (May 2017)

Michael Horsett parachutes into Occupied France before the D-Day Invasion. He is dropped in the wrong place, miles from the action, badly injured, and totally alone. He falls prey to two Thelemist women who have awaited the Hawk God's coming, attracts a group of First World War veterans who rally to what they imagine is his cause, is hunted by a troop of German Field Police who are desperate to find him, and has a climactic encounter with a mutilated priest who believes that Lucifer Incarnate has arrived…

The Lightbearer is a unique gnostic thriller, dealing with the themes of Light and Darkness, Good and Evil, Matter and Spirit.

"The Lightbearer is another shining example of Alan Richardson's talent as a story-teller. He uses his wide esoteric knowledge to produce a story that thrills, chills and startles the reader as it radiates pure magical energy. An unusual and gripping war story with more facets than a star sapphire." – Mélusine Draco, author of "Aubry's Dog" and "Black Horse, White Horse". ISBN: 978-1-907737-63-3 £11.99 $18.99

Dark in the Day, Ed. by Storm Constantine & Paul Houghton

Weirdness lurks beyond the margins of the mundane, emerging to dismantle our assumptions of reality. Dark in the Day is an anthology of weird fiction, penned by established writers and also those new to the genre – the latter being authors who are, or were, students of Creative Writing at Staffordshire University, where editor Storm Constantine occasionally delivers guest lectures. Her co-editor, Paul Houghton, is the senior lecturer in Creative Writing at the university.

Contributors include: Martina Bellovičová, J. E. Bryant, Glynis Charlton, Storm Constantine, Louise Coquio, Elizabeth Counihan, Krishan Coupland, Elizabeth Davidson, Siân Davies, Paul Finch, Rosie Garland, Rhys Hughes, Kerry Fender, Andrew Hook, Paul Houghton, Tanith Lee, Tim Pratt, Nicholas Royle, Michael Marshall Smith, Paula Wakefield, Ian Whates and Liz Williams. ISBN: 978-1-907737-74-9 £11.99, $18.99

Blood, the Phoenix and a Rose by Storm Constantine

Wraeththu, a race of androgynous beings, have arisen from the ashes of human civilisation. Like the mythical rebis, the divine hermaphrodite, they represent the pinnacle of human evolution. But Wraeththu – or hara – were forged in the crucible of destruction and emerged from a new Dark Age. They have yet to realise their full potential and come to terms with the most blighted aspects of their past. Blood, the Phoenix and a Rose begins with an enigma: Gavensel, a har who appears unearthly and has a shrouded history. He has been hidden away in the house of Sallow Gandaloi by Melisander, an alchemist, but is this seclusion to protect Gavensel from the world or the world from him? As his story unfolds, the shadow of the dark fortress Fulminir falls over him, and memories of his past slowly return. The only way to find the truth is to go back through the layers of time, to when the blood was fresh. ISBN: 978-1-907737-75-6 £11.99, $18.99

Animate Objects by Tanith Lee

There is no such thing as an inanimate object… And how could that be? Because, simply, everything is formed from matter, and basically, at *root*, the matter that makes up everything in the physical world – the Universe – is of the same substance. Which means, on that basic level, we – you, me, and that power station over there – are all the exact riotous, chaotic, amorphous *same*. Here is an assortment of Lee takes on the nature, and perhaps intentions, of so-called non-sentient things. And you're quite safe. This is only a book. An inanimate object.

From the Introduction by Tanith Lee

The original hardback of this collection, of which there were only 35 copies, was published by Immanion Press in 2013, to commemorate Tanith Lee receiving the Lifetime Achievement Award at World Fantasycon. It included 5 previously unpublished pieces. This new release includes a further 2 stories, co-written by Tanith Lee and John Kaiine, and new interior illustrations by Jarod Mills. ISBN: 978-1-907737-73-2, £11.99 $18.99

Immanion Press
http://www.immanion-press.com
info@immanion-press.com

NEWCON PRESS

http://newconpress.co.uk/

The very best in fantasy, science fiction, and horror

The Ion Raider by Ian Whates

As Corbin Drake receives his most unusual assignment for First Solar yet – one which he suspects is a trap but knows he can't refuse – his former crew, the notorious brigands known as the Dark Angels, are being hunted down one by one and murdered. Determined to find those responsible before they find her, Leesa teams up with Jen, another former Dark Angel, and together they set out to thwart the mysterious organization known as Saflik, little dreaming where that path will lead them.

ISBN: 978-1-910935-38-5 £12.99 paperback (Also in signed limited edition hardback)

Entropic Angel by Gareth L Powell

Award-winning science fiction writer Gareth L. Powell delivers his first collection in nearly a decade. Gathering together twenty stories, including four that are previously unpublished as well as some of the author's best-loved tales, the content provides highlights from across twelve years of his career, delivering a powerful collection that is both entertaining and thought-provoking.

ISBN: 978-1-910935-42-2 paperback £12.99 (Also in signed limited edition hardback)

www.ingramcontent.com/pod-product-compliance
Lightning Source LLC
Chambersburg PA
CBHW030119260626
47156CB00008B/2723